T0346256

Maurice Procter and The Murder Room

>>> This title is part of The Murder Room, our series dedicated to making available out-of-print or hard-to-find titles by classic crime writers.

Crime fiction has always held up a mirror to society. The Victorians were fascinated by sensational murder and the emerging science of detection; now we are obsessed with the forensic detail of violent death. And no other genre has so captivated and enthralled readers.

Vast troves of classic crime writing have for a long time been unavailable to all but the most dedicated frequenters of second-hand bookshops. The advent of digital publishing means that we are now able to bring you the backlists of a huge range of titles by classic and contemporary crime writers, some of which have been out of print for decades.

From the genteel amateur private eyes of the Golden Age and the femmes fatales of pulp fiction, to the morally ambiguous hard-boiled detectives of mid twentieth-century America and their descendants who walk our twenty-first century streets, The Murder Room has it all. >>>

The Murder Room
Where Criminal Minds Meet

themurderroom.com

Maurice Procter 1906–1973

Born in Nelson, Lancashire, Maurice Procter attended the local grammar school and ran away to join the army at the age of fifteen. In 1927 he joined the police in Yorkshire and served in the force for nineteen years before his writing was published and he was able to write full-time. He was credited with an ability to write exciting stories while using his experience to create authentic detail. His procedural novels are set in Granchester, a fictional 1950s Manchester, and he is best known for his series characters, Detective Superintendent Philip Hunter and DCI Harry Martineau. Throughout his career, Procter's novels increased in popularity in both the UK and the US, and in 1960 *Hell is a City* was made into a film starring Stanley Baker and Billie Whitelaw. Procter was married to Winifred, and they had one child, Noel.

Philip Hunter

The Chief Inspector's Statement (1951)
  aka *The Pennycross Murders*
I Will Speak Daggers (1956)
  aka *The Ripper*

Chief Inspector Martineau

Hell is a City (1954)
  aka *Somewhere in This City*
The Midnight Plumber (1957)
Man in Ambush (1958)
Killer at Large (1959)

Devil's Due (1960)
The Devil Was Handsome (1961)
A Body to Spare (1962)
Moonlight Flitting (1963)
   aka *The Graveyard Rolls*
Two Men in Twenty (1964)
Homicide Blonde (1965)
   aka *Death has a Shadow*
His Weight in Gold (1966)
Rogue Running (1966)
Exercise Hoodwink (1967)
Hideaway (1968)

Standalone Novels
Each Man's Destiny (1947)
No Proud Chivalry (1947)
The End of the Street (1949)
Hurry the Darkness (1952)
Rich is the Treasure (1952)
   aka *Diamond Wizard*
The Pub Crawler (1956)
Three at the Angel (1958)
The Spearhead Death (1960)
Devil in Moonlight (1962)
The Dog Man (1969)

A Body to Spare

Maurice Procter

An Orion book

Copyright © Maurice Procter 1962

The right of Maurice Procter to be identified as the author of this work
has been asserted in accordance with the Copyright, Designs and Patents
Act 1988.

This edition published by
The Orion Publishing Group Ltd
Orion House
5 Upper St Martin's Lane
London WC2H 9EA

An Hachette UK company
A CIP catalogue record for this book is available from the British Library

ISBN 978 1 4719 0275 8

All characters and events in this publication are fictitious and any
resemblance to real people, living or dead, is purely coincidental.

No part of this publication may be reproduced, stored in a retrieval system
or transmitted in any form or by any means without the prior permission
in writing of the publisher, nor be otherwise circulated in any form of
binding or cover other than that in which it is published without a similar
condition, including this condition, being imposed on the subsequent
purchaser.

www.orionbooks.co.uk

ONE

ON THE internal-line telephone, Detective Chief Superintendent Clay's voice sounded testy. "You'd better nip round to the morgue at the General Hospital," he growled. "They find they've got a body too many."

Detective Chief Inspector Martineau was taken by surprise. "A what?"

"Body. Unaccounted for. Some damn silly mistake. Go clear it up."

Martineau shrugged as he put down the receiver. He did not see how a mistake by a mortuary attendant could be a C.I.D. affair, but the order to see to it had been definite enough. He rose from his chair and reached for his hat. The reach was a long one, across the desk to the top of a bookcase where the hat had been thrown. It was achieved without strain. Martineau was a very big man, with powerful shoulders and large hands. At one time he had been the hardest hitter among the eleven hundred men of a city police force noted for the physique of its members. Now, a little over forty years of age, he was still formidable.

He carelessly clapped the hat onto a head of fair hair with some gray in it. The face beneath the hat was rather handsome, in a weathered sort of way. Though he was a city man, some

1

quality of his blood gave him the complexion of a huntsman.

He strode from his own small sanctum into the long room of the main C.I.D. office. Detective Sergeant Devery and Detective Constable Cassidy were there, numbering and checking items of stolen property recently found in the home of a shoplifter who had committed suicide.

"Drop that," Martineau said as he passed the place where they were working at the long main desk.

Cassidy said, "Lady's crocodile handbag, brown, with gold-colored clasp." Devery said, "Twenty-nine." He wrote the number, then two documents were hastily slipped into two adjacent drawers. By the time Martineau reached the police station yard, the sergeant and the constable were at his heels.

"Where are we going, sir?" asked Devery, as the three of them climbed into the plain C.I.D. car which was set aside for Martineau's own use.

"Hospital. They've got too many bodies," was the answer. It was not given curtly, but Devery asked no further question. It was evident to him that Martineau had no more to tell.

At the Granchester General Hospital they drove round to the mortuary. An attendant was waiting in the doorway of the grim brick building. The three tall men got out of the car. Though they were of different physical types, each carried the impalpable yet clearly perceptible aura of his profession. In a manner in which excitement was restrained by deference, the attendant turned his head and called through the doorway, "They're here, sir."

Martineau led the way into the mortuary. He was surprised to see that the chief pathologist was there, with two young doctors. He realized that the "mistake," whatever it was, must be a matter of some importance.

The pathologist was a great man in his own sphere. He had a manner. He indicated the uncovered and completely naked body of a man, which lay on a slab. "No problem with this one," he said without preamble. "He's been medically and officially examined, found dead, inquested and cremated. And he's still with us. Dr. Provis here can identify him."

Martineau began to perceive what had happened. He made up his mind to have the affair on a proper footing from the start.

2

"That won't do for me," he said. "Dr. Provis could be mistaken. I want a second formal identification by a near relative."

"Ah, now medicine bows its head to the law," said the pathologist. But instead of bowing his head he raised it thoughtfully, looking at a high window. He was there in person because of a fantastically unusual occurrence, that was all. Only the legal side of the affair was left. There was *no* medical side. That had been charred to ashes and scattered in the wind.

Having perceived that there was nothing more to say except good-by, he said it and departed. There was a general air of relief among those who remained.

"Now then," said Martineau. "Which of you gentlemen is Dr. Provis?"

Provis was a handsome young medico with an attractive grin. "It was my case, such as it was," he stated.

Martineau nodded, and reflected that this was a lad who would create havoc among the nurses. He moved to the body and looked at it. "My word," he said. "He took a beating."

Provis explained: "It was an accident in a timber yard. He was driving a truck. He stopped his truck in the wrong place, and had just climbed out when a craneload of heavy planks came swinging round and hit the truck. Unfortunately his head was caught between the timber and the truck."

"Mmmm. Death instantaneous?"

"I suppose so. He certainly was dead when he arrived here."

"And there was an inquest?"

"Yes. Accidental death."

"And a report in the papers?"

"Yes. There was one in the local evening paper, at any rate. I read it myself."

"What was the man's name?"

"Edgar Waite."

"And after the supposed cremation, where was he found?"

Provis looked at the mortuary attendant. "Speak up, Briggs," he said.

"I found him down there in Number Twelve box," said Briggs. "It's one we don't use until we're full up."

"How did you come to find it?"

"We was empty, sir. Not a single body in. It sometimes happens like that for an hour or two. But I happened to notice the meter tickin' over, an' I thought I'd better investigate. I didn't expect to find a body, though."

"What did you expect to find?"

"I dunno. Sometimes the young doctors an' even the nurses get up to their tricks. It mighter been a dead cat, or summat like that."

"Was there any identification on the body?"

"None at all."

"What identification should there be?"

"A label tied to the wrist, one stuck on the leg, an' one on the shroud. There was no label on the body, an' no shroud."

"Did you recognize the body?"

"Not for sure. I see so many. Dr. Provis recognized it."

Provis interposed. "I remembered it. And I checked my notes to the exact nature of the injuries. It's Waite, all right."

"Mmmm. How long has he been under refrigeration?"

"Well, he came in last Wednesday, and he was identified and examined on Thursday. The inquest was on Friday. He was on ice then till Monday morning, when some undertaker came and put him in a coffin, and he was cremated Monday afternoon. Yesterday, that is."

"You mean *somebody* was cremated yesterday."

"Of course. Sometime between Thursday evening and Monday morning Waite was stripped of his labels and moved from Number Five to Number Twelve. We checked everything before we called the police. There has been no clerical error. The only thing we can suppose is that sometime between Thursday and Monday the body of an unknown person was put in Waite's place, with Waite's shroud and Waite's labels, and was eventually cremated with due ceremony in Waite's name."

"Friday, Saturday, Sunday," Martineau muttered. Then he asked, "Is this place locked at night?"

Provis did not look at Briggs when he answered. "It's supposed to be locked at any time when there is no one in attendance, but in practice I doubt if it is ever locked. It's a busy place, you know. New arrivals at all times of day and night. Quite often the attendant has to go into a ward and bring out a body, and he doesn't bother to lock up for the short time he's away."

"Wasn't it likely that the substitution would be discovered before the cremation? Some near relation might have wanted to take a last look at poor Edgar."

"Not in his condition. Once he was identified, no relation would want to take another look. And if the body which was substituted also had severe head injuries, it isn't likely that any of the mortuary staff would notice."

"The substitution wouldn't take long?"

"Not if the people concerned knew whose body they were going to move. Just a few minutes, I'd say."

"And they could have known if there had been a report in the paper."

"Yes. So you see how it could become a job for the police?"

"I do indeed. Somebody wanting to get rid of a body with a battered head. Murder or manslaughter."

"Somebody might be missing from home."

"Somebody is," said Martineau dryly. "Somebody certainly is. We've been seeking him for the last two days."

Back at Police Headquarters, Martineau initiated certain inquiries. Taking nothing for granted, he instructed Devery to go carefully over the case of Edgar Waite's accidental death and instructed Cassidy to see the Waite family and arrange a second formal identification of the body. He also sent out other members of his staff on other inquiries. The supposed murder or manslaughter could have been a mob killing, and he wanted to know if any hooligan or criminal was missing from his usual haunts. He also wanted a check on local men recently let out of jail, to be sure that they were alive and well. He also ordered a closer scrutiny of the normal list of runaway sons, runaway husbands, military absentees, and absconding offenders.

All that was routine, and when he had arranged it Martineau sat in his office and meditated upon the disappearance of (a) £29,000 and (b) a man called Verney Barton. Though they had not disappeared together, the two items were connected. Barton was, or had been, the head wages clerk of the enormous Northern Steel Corporation, and the £29,000 had been the payroll of one of Northern Steel's mills. The cash had been lost sight of on Friday morning, and Barton had vanished on Saturday night. Now it was Tuesday morning, and there had been so few leads to either the money or Barton that Devery and Cassidy, Martineau's right and left hands, were still messing about with small items of Property Recovered.

The chief inspector marveled that even now, when British crooks had realized how easy it was to seize money in transit, and when big payroll snatches were occurring daily, men carrying large sums of money were caught napping, and unarmed. In spite of the holdups so frequently reported in the daily papers, the possibility of attack and financial bereavement still seemed to be remote; something that "happened in the paper," to other people. The four men carrying the Northern Steel money had been a burly but elderly driver, two husky young members of the firm's office staff, and small, spare, forty-five-year-old Verney, the man in charge. Their vehicle had been an ordinary saloon car, and they had gone to the bank for the wages at eleven o'clock on Friday morning as they had always done. To confuse the enemy Verney had two routes. If he went to the bank by No. 1 route he always returned by No. 2 route, or the other way round. So, thieves who had been studying the situation had only to watch him go to know which way he was coming back.

Martineau calculated that the Northern Steel holdup had been perpetrated by six men, or at the most seven. They had been masked. There had been four club men armed with lengths of heavy lead piping, and two or possibly three wheel men. There had been nothing original in the method of attack. A large fast van—stolen—had been skillfully maneuvered so that it "accidentally" blocked the way of the payroll car on the quietest part of the return journey. From the flank a three-tonner—also illegally borrowed—had rammed the car so violently that one of the driver's legs had been broken. The club men had poured out of the van and attacked the crew of the car. Having no time to waste, they had pulled Verney out into the road, tapped him on the head, and forgotten him. They had shattered every window of the car in a successful effort to get their clubs to the heads of the two men on the back seat. The youngsters had fought well with their fists, and as a reward for their resistance each had suffered a fractured skull. The driver also had been hit on the head, because he had tried to obstruct the thieves in spite of his broken leg. Only Verney had been comparatively uninjured.

Though noisy, the encounter had been remarkably brief. Well trained in their parts, the thieves had got the whole of the Northern Steel payroll into their van and had piled in after it. Later the van had been found abandoned and, with regard to fingerprints, as clean as a whistle.

Because of his slight injuries, of the four guardians of the payroll Verney was the one most closely interrogated.

"Were you knocked out of time?" Martineau asked him.

"No," Verney replied without hesitation, "but after I was hit I lay where I fell, acting dead."

"Why?"

"So's they'd leave me alone, and I could give the alarm straight away when they'd gone."

"Didn't it occur to you to get up and help your friends?"

"Against those fellows? They were all three times as big as me. I wouldn't have lasted half a minute."

"Did you recognize any of them?"

"No. Not yet."

"What do you mean by 'not yet'?"

"I kept my eyes open when they weren't looking my way. I keep trying to remember things about them."

"Do keep trying," Martineau said.

That was the substance of the interview. Naturally, the police did not overlook the possibility that Verney was in league with the thieves. Inquiries were made with regard to the sort of life he led when he was not studying time sheets. It was found that he was a gay dog, in a harmless sort of way. On the evenings when he could escape from his own fireside he spent his time in places where adventurous girls could be found. There was some likelihood, but no proof, that he had been spending more money than a man in his position could afford.

So, when Verney's worried wife reported that he was missing, Martineau got out of bed and went to take charge of the search of his house. Only one item of interest was found: a curious item, hidden in an amateurish way. Martineau carefully replaced it in its hiding place and made no comment about it to members of Verney's family.

7

Verney's wife reported him missing at three o'clock in the morning of the Sunday following the robbery, because, she said, he had never stayed out so late before. Since that time he had not been heard of, or seen.

And now, on Tuesday morning, when it could be assumed that Martineau was up to his neck in the investigation of the Northern Steel job, Clay had instructed the chief inspector to go personally to the General Hospital with regard to a body. Actually, that instruction should have been given to the coroner's officer. But Clay had not put into words any thought that a body at the hospital might have some connection with the Northern Steel job.

Nevertheless, the thought must have been in his mind. Had it not been, he would not have sent a busy senior officer to the hospital.

"Happen he's guessing right," Martineau mused. "It's the first thing I thought of, too. It could be that Mr. Verney Barton is now a cinder."

TWO

WHETHER or not the Northern Steel case and the Spare Body job were connected, Clay showed no intention of putting the files of either onto the desk of any other officer. Martineau had them both, and he was not consulted as to his wishes in the matter.

But there were other consultations, and after discussion it was decided that the Spare Body affair was a case in which publicity would be more important than usual. Because the coroner had stated that a second inquest on Edgar Waite would not be necessary, it might have been possible to keep the matter out of the papers. The hospital authorities wanted it so, but the police were compelled to have it otherwise because of their great need for information. Clay issued a statement which was cunningly designed to arouse the interest of newspapermen by allowing them to draw their own conclusions. He did not suggest that there was any connection between Verney Barton and the unknown person who had been cremated. He knew very well that the press would soon do that for him. The press did, and the headlines grew.

While he waited for the spate of letters, phone calls, and direct visitations which would be the public reaction to newspaper reports, Martineau directed a last-minute probe of the city's underworld. Tomorrow his men would be busy following up hundreds of items of information, most of them useless. Tonight they could harass known wrongdoers or listen quietly to the hoarse whispers of informers. The informers were on the lookout for flash money, and lavish spending was not the only sign of it. A thief can betray a state of unusual affluence merely by being seen with the wrong sort of woman—the sort he cannot normally afford.

And Martineau was uneasily aware that it was not only the police who were watching for signs of flash money. While £29,000 was not the biggest tickle in the world, it was big enough to excite the envy of professional mobsters. In Granchester there were certain individual criminals and groups of criminals who would be even more anxious than the police to know what had happened to the Northern Steel plunder. And those people had sources of information which were denied the police. Dog eat dog. If any of them found the money, they would take it in a lightning raid, and that could make the business of finding it much more difficult for the police.

The following day the story of the Spare Body was prominent on the front page of every national daily, and late in the afternoon, in the working-class suburb of Bearsdyke, a woman stopped a uniformed P.C. in the street. She stated that she and her husband had heard some commotion late on Saturday night, on the site of a building which would be a petrol filling station when it was finished.

"It were a fight of some sort," the woman said. "I wanted to 'ave a look, but me 'usband said it were Teddy Boys very likely, an' we'd better keep away. So we went on 'ome. But wi' seein' that thing in the paper I thought, 'Eeh, I wonder.' "

The constable's name was Joe Ainslie. He was one of the bigger sort of bobbies, and he was young, smart and very serious about his work.

"What time was this, madam?" he asked.

" 'Appen about ten past eleven. We'd been 'avin' an hour at the Griffin, like we do every Sat'day night. We sat talkin' for a while after closin' time, then we come 'ome. Yes, it 'ud be about ten past when we were passin' the new garridge."

Ainslie knew all about the new filling station. He had watched

10

its construction from the laying of the foundations and the digging of the tank pits. He remembered now that the walls had been built, but that there were as yet only rectangular holes for doors and windows, and the gray Granchester sky for a roof. A fight in there? It was likely enough.

"Do you mean the place with the sign 'Dykeside Garage'?" he asked, just to be sure.

"That's it."

"Did you see *anything* of the disturbance?"

"No. I can't see through a brick wall."

"What did you hear?"

"Thumps an' grunts and groans. An' somebody cursin'."

"Quite loudly?"

"No. I couldn't 'ear any words, but it was cursin'."

"Did your husband hear it more clearly?"

"Not 'im. 'Is ears aren't as good as mine."

"I see. Would you tell me your name?"

The woman did not try to conceal her dismay. She had yearned to tell some official about the trouble at the filling station, and now that she had done so she remembered that it was one thing her husband had forbidden her to do.

"I'd rather not give me name," she said.

Ainslie could have let the woman go, and made a note that she had declined to give her name. Normally he would have done so. The thing was probably a false alarm anyway. But she had mentioned the Spare Body job. Possibly that was simply because she had been excited by newspaper headlines. And possibly it was because she knew a little more than she had told.

"You've read the papers. There might have been a murder Saturday night," he said. "You come to me and make a report. You may turn out to be an important witness. You'd better tell me your name."

The last words were a piece of advice uttered in the tone of a command. "Oh dear," the woman said. "It's Lockyer. Mrs. Vera Lockyer."

"And the address?"

She gave her address, and her husband's name and occupation. "Thank you," said Ainslie. "Someone may come along to take a statement from you." He closed his pocketbook and bade Mrs.

11

Lockyer good morning, and turned away. Rather disconsolately the woman resumed her homeward journey. When she had gone a little way Ainslie turned again and followed her, thus discreetly making sure that she did go to the address she had given.

P. C. Ainslie's next duty was to "ring in" the information to his division, where it would come under the heading of a Suspicious Occurrence. "I don't know whether it's worth putting through to the C.I.D.," he concluded.

"They're run off their feet already," said the clerk at Div. H.Q.

"All right. Make a marginal note. Attention by B. 182 Ainslie."

"Right," said the clerk. "You'll be engaged for—how long?"

"Oh, an hour. If there is anything, I'll take a statement to round it off."

"Right," the clerk repeated, and Ainslie made his way to Dykeside Garage. He walked briskly, but without haste. In his six years' service he had attended many occurrences which had promised excitement and ended with a commonplace explanation. But he had a sanguine nature. "You never know," he told himself. "This might be it."

As he walked, Ainslie remembered that there had been no men working on the building site when he had passed it earlier that morning. And, now that the memory might be important, he recalled that the site had also been deserted on Monday and Tuesday. No doubt there had been some hitch, to do with finance probably, which had made the contractor withdraw his men. It was possible that there had been nobody on the premises since Saturday night.

As he stepped over the threshold of a doorless doorway Ainslie thought about the weather of the last few days. It had been typical of early April in that region, cold and dull, with very little rain. The interior of the roofless building was quite dry. The concrete floor was gritty with builder's sand and littered with broken bricks, trowel droppings, and other debris of the trade. The path made by dirty boots from doorway to doorway could be clearly seen.

P. C. Ainslie moved around. There were, or would be, four main rooms in the single-story building. He presumed, by their size in relation to each other, that they would be showroom, office, repair shop and storeroom. In the back part of the building, in a corner of the repair shop, he found what he was looking for. There was a space which might have been swept clean of debris by scuffling feet. On the concrete were a number of dark-brown spots and smears. One of these was very large, and Ainslie assumed that the head of a dying man had lain there while his assailants were deciding what to do with him.

Keeping his large, glossy boots well clear of the scene of the "commotion," the policeman squatted and peered at the rubbish on the perimeter of the cleared space. There were some broken bricks. He carefully picked up the ones within reach, and then as carefully replaced them. None of them seemed to be blood-stained. Well, some handier weapon than a brick might have been used.

He got up and made for the street, conscious that he dared not leave his discovery unguarded. If he went away for ten minutes or so, the reverse side of his lucky seam might bring along a gang of rowdy boys to make a mess of things. He stood on the edge of the site until a responsible person came along. This happened to be a bus driver, off duty, whom he knew by sight.

"How do," said the bus driver as he was passing.

"How do. In a terrible hurry, mate?"

The bus driver frowned. Was this bobby going to start questioning him, who was well known to be an honest man?

"I'm goin' somewhere," he said. "But I'm not runnin', am I?"

Ainslie grinned. "Do me a favor. Stop at that phone box on the corner of Parkin Street and dial nine-nine-nine. Give your name and ask for police and tell 'em P. C. Ainslie requires assistance at the new garage site in Dykeside. That's all."

The bus driver looked at the outwardly unruffled officer and then peered past him at the incomplete building. "Assistance?" he queried.

"Right. And I'm not kidding," the P. C. replied. He jerked a thumb over his shoulder. "It's in there and I daren't leave it."

The bus driver was impressed. Happen another body had been found. Well, if the bobby had wanted to broadcast such a discovery he would have said so. So it was no use asking.

"I'll tell 'em," he said, and he went on his way at a quicker pace.

Ainslie waited five minutes, during which time he went five

13

times to see that his find was undisturbed. Then an Area Patrol car arrived, with a crew of two. Ainslie knew the two very well. If it were a matter of taking credit for police work, they would steal a blind man's last penny. Joe's excitement mounted. Here was competition. If he left these two in charge while he went to a telephone to contact Division, they would nose around and find the blood and then perhaps they would get ahead of him by going straight through to H.Q. by radio. He wouldn't put it past them.

"Now then, Joe me lad," the driver called cheerfully as the car stopped. "What's up? Somebody been hittin' you?"

This was Donny Styles, a proper bastard in Joe Ainslie's opinion. But he also spoke lightly as he replied, "All I want is for one of you two birds to get off his arse for a change, so's I can use your radio."

"I'll put your message through," said Styles kindly. "What is it?"

The driver's mate was an intelligent, ruthless Scot called Armstrong, born to achieve high rank in whatever profession he chose to take up. He got out of the car and was striding purposefully past Joe when the beat man reached out and caught his arm.

"So far and no farther," he said. "I'm senior to you by six months, and them's my orders."

Armstrong appraised him coolly. "I don't take orders from you," he said.

"Please yourself then. But if you go in there you'll drop a clanger. I'll see to it you do. I'm telling you straight."

Armstrong thought that over. "I don't drop clangers either," he said, and he returned to the car with Joe.

"Now don't waste any more of my time," Joe said firmly to Styles. "Put me through and let me give my message."

"This boy hasn't had his cooling powder today," Styles grumbled, but he made the contact with Headquarters.

The opposition had increased Joe's determination to make the most of his luck. Since he had been compelled to bypass his own division and speak to Headquarters, he decided that he would get into touch with the man who mattered. To the clerk in the Information Room he said, "This is B. 182 Ainslie. I have an urgent and personal message for Chief Inspector Martineau. I

14

am speaking from the site of an incomplete garage in Dykeside. There is evidence which requires his personal attention, and it is evidence which might be impaired or destroyed if anybody starts blundering about."

"Evidence of what?"

"Of grievous bodily harm, at the very least. This message is from B. 182 Ainslie."

"I got the name," said the clerk coolly. "I'll pass your message on to Sergeant Devery."

"You'll pass it on to Martineau if you don't want to be blown right off that buffet. And you'll do it now."

"Brave words, boy. You're on the crest of a wave, hey? I hope you don't find yourself all washed up. Hold on a minute."

And just about a minute later the reply came. "He's on his way. Look out for yourself, kid."

"Thanks," said Joe, as he relinquished the microphone to Styles, and with sarcasm, "I'll do the same for you sometime."

There followed an argument between Styles and Armstrong. The Scot wanted to stay. He wanted to have a hand in the thing, whatever it was. But Styles was the driver and the senior man. "I know Martineau," he said. "If he sees us at all he'll ask us what we're hanging about here for." And he started his engine and drove off.

So, after much anxiety and not too much delay, P. C. Ainslie was left alone to enjoy his triumph, if triumph it was to be. He had waited six years for an opportunity of this sort, and he was satisfied that he had exploited it fully. He was also in some fear that he had exploited it too much if it should turn out to be a matter of no importance.

Well, it was worth the risk. The achievement of recognition in a police force was just as much a rat race as it was in any other organization. Push your luck and trust nobody, that was the rule. Perhaps Joe had been a little too anxious to push his luck, but if his effort put Martineau on to a good line of inquiry, the chief inspector would request his services for C.I.D. work until the job was cleared. He nearly always did that, because he also liked to follow up a lucky break.

THREE

MARTINEAU arrived with horse, foot and artillery; that is to say, with Sergeant Bird and three of his men, and a vanload of equipment for the gathering and preserving of evidence in all its material forms.

As he got out of his car he looked keenly at the waiting constable, and his mood was not apparent to the anxious young man. "Ainslie?" he asked.

"Yes, sir."

"Show me. Bird, you wait out here a moment."

Joe showed him, then told him Mrs. Lockyer's story.

"Mmmm," he said. Then he squatted as Joe had done. Then he said, "You've done very well, Ainslie. Let us hope it's what we think it is. Now, go and stand at the front and see that nobody comes in here."

When the elated but outwardly solemn P. C. had left him, Martineau moved back from the scene of conflict and squatted again, and at an oblique angle he discerned a vague footprint in the floor's powdering of sand. It looked like the print of a rubber sole with a ribbed tread. Good. Bird would put a light on that and photograph it from various angles. He would "freeze" it and might even get some sort of impression. He would find other footprints if they were there. A valuable man was Bird.

The chief inspector stood up and looked around. He could not see the weapon. Half bricks were not good enough for the sort of damage he had in mind. He looked through a window orifice at the ground behind the building. It looked promising. There was a huge heap of bricks, not yet neatly piled but lying anyhow as they had slid from a tip-up truck. He called Bird and his men and set them to work inside the building. Then he went out the back way and stood looking at the bricks.

"Ainslie!" he shouted, and the constable appeared.

"We'll inspect a few of these bricks," Martineau said. "A whole brick might have been used, and then thrown on this heap."

"Yes, sir," said Joe, and he stooped and picked up a brick which was lying at his feet. He turned it over and stared at it in silence for a moment, then he said, "This is the one, I think."

Martineau came to look. The brick was stained on two sides, as if the edge had cut open somebody's scalp. A few hairs adhered to it.

"Well, that beats cockfighting," he said in delight. "First time. This *is* your lucky day."

"Shall I examine the other bricks, sir?"

"Yes, but I won't be heartbroken if you don't find another one. This will do nicely."

Joe bent to the task, starting an orderly pile of bricks. Martineau carried the precious exhibit to his car, then he rejoined Sergeant Bird. "Well?" he asked.

"There were at least three people in here," the sergeant said. He pointed to the footmark which Martineau had already seen. "We can use that one."

"Aren't the others any good?"

"No."

"Will they be able to do anything with the blood?"

"I should think so. It's thick on the ground."

Martineau told him about the brick. "When we searched Barton's house I took a few hairs from his hairbrush, just in case," he said. "I'm going to the lab now, to get a comparison. I'll get them to send somebody out to look at this blood."

He went to the police forensic laboratory, and very soon he

knew that the hairs on the bloodstained brick corresponded in detail with the hairs from Verney Barton's head. He was also moderately sure that Verney was dead.

He returned to the building site with a laboratory assistant, who made a preliminary test and assured him that the blood on the floor was human blood. Satisfied, he went outside and found Ainslie still piling bricks. Of the original heap there were very few left. He helped to examine those few, and as Ainslie picked up the last brick he looked at his watch.

"You're Early Turn, I suppose," he said.

"Yes, sir."

"It's now half past two."

"That's all right, sir. I'm not to half an hour."

"All right, you can go off duty now, and you must tell your inspector that I'm requesting you for temporary C.I.D. work. I'll make the formal request. You'll be at A Div. C.I.D. in plain clothes at nine o'clock tomorrow morning."

"Yes, sir," Joe said, trying hard to conceal his pleasure.

Though Verney Barton had not been a qualified accountant, he had held a good position in the Northern Steel Corporation. His living conditions had reflected this. Though his house was old enough to have seen two world wars, it was well maintained, larger than most, and in a good district. As he walked up to the front door with Devery at his side, Martineau looked at the neat lawn and wondered who would do the gardening now. He thought of the car in the back-yard garage, and wondered who would drive it. He felt sorry for the woman he was going to see. She could not yet be relieved of her anxiety.

When he rang, she answered the door. Her look was a question. He shook his head. "I'm sorry, Mrs. Barton," he said. "No good news yet."

The pale, pretty little woman bowed her head. "Oh dear," she sighed. "I thought you'd brought me news."

"No. I came to ask you to let me look over the house again. There might be something."

"Come in," she said.

As the policemen followed her toward the living room, Anne

18

Barton, daughter of the house, came downstairs. She was a straight-eyed girl of twenty, pretty like her mother, but otherwise not remarkable. Martineau was surprised to see her there, until he remembered that she worked in a department store. Wednesday was early closing day.

"Good afternoon," she said in answer to Martineau's greeting. "I'm glad you came. Mother has something to tell you."

Mrs. Barton turned and looked reproachfully at the girl, but she did not speak.

"You must tell him," Anne insisted. "We have nothing to hide. I *know* Daddy wouldn't do anything dishonest."

They went into the living room. Anne went to a bureau and found a bank passbook. She gave it to Martineau. "My parents have a joint bank account," she said. "They have a current account and a deposit account. They don't use the deposit account much, but a month ago Daddy drew out five hundred pounds without telling Mother. It's there in the book."

Martineau opened the book and looked at the entry. He had seen it, and made a note of it, during the first search of the house. He did not say so.

"He didn't take that money out to run away," Anne said fiercely. "He wouldn't do that."

Martineau smiled. He had never hinted to these people that he had had any suspicion of Verney, and he was glad now that he had not done so. "Your father didn't run away," he said. "I know that."

The girl went white. "Is—is he dead?" she faltered. "Was he that man they cremated?"

"I don't know," the policeman had to say. Someday quite soon there would have to be an attempt to establish a presumption of Verney's death. He had carried quite a lot of insurance, and Northern Steel had a pension scheme for the widows of workers. But Martineau had not yet received permission to say anything to the family.

He said, "I'm sorry I can't tell you anything, but I'm reasonably certain that Mr. Barton didn't run away. I think I know why he withdrew money from the bank, but I mustn't say anything yet. I can only tell you that I believe he invested it quite legitimately."

"Well, that's something," Anne said, but her mother was weeping quietly. Obviously she had made the inference. If Verney had not run away, then he was dead.

"Do you mind if we go up to your bedroom?" Martineau asked.

There was no reply. The girl had moved across the room to comfort her mother. The policemen quietly left the room and went upstairs.

In the master bedroom there was an old-fashioned walnut suite which was still in gleaming condition. Martineau went straight to the wardrobe, which stood with its back to the wall. He opened the door. On the floor of the wardrobe shoes were arranged in a neat line. They were small, but they were a man's shoes.

"It was rolled into a tight wad and stuffed into the toe of a pair of winkle pickers," he said, stooping over the shoes. "Ah, here they are."

He picked up one of a pair of sharply pointed pumps, of the sort worn with evening dress.

"Patent leather," Devery commented. "Just the job for finger-prints."

"Yes," Martineau replied. "I'll be careful, just in case."

His big fingers explored the inside of one shoe, and then the other. He shook his head. "It's gone."

"Well, an experienced tea leaf wouldn't have much of a job finding it, would he?"

"Not if he was looking for that particular thing. Verney wasn't hiding it from a thief, he was hiding it from his wife. There aren't many women who clean their husbands' shoes. Very likely Verney's wife never touched his."

"So what do we do now?"

"We'll have to go over the entire house again, just to be sure. You be doing this room, starting with the shoes, while I go down and have another word with the women."

The chief inspector went down to the living room, and was relieved to find that Mrs. Barton was no longer weeping. "I must ask you something," he said. "Has anybody touched Mr. Barton's shoes since Saturday?"

Both women stared in surprise. Then Anne looked at her

mother. That lady shook her head. "I haven't touched them at all."

"I haven't either," Anne said.

"Have you had a cleaning woman in the place?"

"No. She left a fortnight ago, and we haven't got another one yet."

"Mmmm. I noticed that you took the chain off the front door when you opened it today. Do you always have it on the chain?"

"Yes, ever since somebody sneaked in and took an overcoat and a raincoat belonging to my husband. They were in the hall cupboard."

"What about the back door?"

"We keep that locked. What's the matter, has somebody taken a pair of Verney's shoes?"

"They've taken something which was hidden in a shoe. How many times has the house been left unoccupied since Saturday?"

"I haven't been out since Saturday. Anne has been doing the shopping, such as it was."

Anne interposed. "You have been out, Mother. We went to church on Sunday morning. We *always* go to church on Sunday, and last Sunday we went specially."

"Is Verney a churchgoer too?" he asked curiously.

"No," Anne replied. "He never would go."

"How long were you out of the house on Sunday?"

"From ten to ten till about twenty past eleven," Anne replied promptly.

"And the house was deserted?"

"Yes."

"And you don't think it's possible for anyone to have been in the house at any other time?"

"I don't think so. Mother would have known. She was very good hearing, even when she's asleep."

Martineau went to look at the back door. It had a small modern latch, but it was deadlocked. No thief could have opened it without making a noise and leaving a mark. He looked at the two kitchen windows. They were of the sash type which could not be opened silently. The catches were of the old-fashioned screw type which could only be negotiated from the outside by breaking the glass or by using a thin hacksaw. When he ex-

21

amined the second window he found that the thief had used a hacksaw. The bar of the catch was cleanly cut in two, and the filings had been carefully swept away.

He opened and closed the window, and heard the noise it made. Then he returned to the living room. "Did you hear anything?" he asked Mrs. Barton.

"You opened a window, and closed it again."

"Would you have heard that if you had been asleep in bed?"

"I certainly would. I'm nervous of burglars."

"Would you wake up if someone came into your bedroom while you were asleep?"

Mrs. Barton hesitated. Her daughter said, "Of course she would. I remember once creeping in to get the aspirins. I knew exactly where they were and I didn't make a sound. But she woke up."

Martineau was satisfied. Someone had entered the house on Sunday morning, and at no other time. He had taken a document—a small sheet of notepaper—from Verney's shoe. He had looked in the shoe and in similar places, because he had known that Verney had hidden it from his wife, who was unaware of its existence. He had taken the document because he knew that Verney was dead.

Martineau took Anne out into the hall and showed her the two halves of the little steel bar. "You had a thief in on Sunday morning, by the kitchen window," he said. "I'm going to bring in a crew of men to search the house thoroughly. One of them will make the window secure, for the time being."

The girl thanked him. Watching her closely, he asked, "Do you happen to know a man called Gerry Gee?"

"The night club man? No. I've heard of him, but I've never seen him."

"Does your mother know him?"

"No, I'm sure she doesn't. She's heard of him of course. Nearly everybody has. Why?"

"Just something I had to ask. Don't bother your head about it, and don't tell your mother."

He left her then, and went upstairs to Devery. That young man was busy, with his coat off.

"Look," said the chief inspector, showing his two pieces of

22

steel. "Kitchen window. And it had to be Sunday morning while the family was at church."

Devery stopped work to think about that. "Very interesting," he said. "Verney invests five hundred pounds in the Gee Gee Club, and he's ashamed to tell his wife. He hides the contract—or share certificate, if you like—in the toe of a shoe. That contract was there after Verney was reported missing in the small hours of Sunday morning. We think he was killed a few hours before that. Before it was generally known that Verney wasn't around the homestead any more, somebody broke in here and pinched the contract. It was of value only to Verney or his estate, but it also had a sort of value to Gerry Gee if he could get hold of it and destroy it. Look after those shoes, guvnor. Gerry may have taken his gloves off to get that bit of paper out."

"Let us hope so," said Martineau. He frowned. "I never thought of Gee as a violent man."

"No. But he has violent friends. I could name one or two."

"Anyway, at eleven o'clock Sunday morning he knew Verney Barton was dead. If that wasn't guilty knowledge you can call me Crippen. Gerry's the boy for me."

Devery reached for his coat. "Do we go and get him?"

"Tonight," said Martineau. "He doesn't yet know we're looking his way. We'll gather a bit of material for his biography before we move in on him."

FOUR

IT WAS generally understood in Granchester that the Gee Gee Club was a profitable concern, and but for one factor Verney Barton's investment might have been regarded as a sound one. The factor in question was the character of the owner or chief shareholder. Gerry Gee was a tall, handsome man of great affability and charm. He had been partner or proprietor in many upstart ventures, all of which had failed. They had failed because prosperity always brought a recurrence of fever in him, a fever to invest money in the industry which supports horses and jockeys. In short, G. Gee could not carry corn.

Chief Inspector Martineau knew that Gerry owed much money in the town, but it is not against the law to fail in business, or to borrow money and dissipate it, and he had been inclined to regard the man as harmless. But on that Wednesday evening in April he looked at him very grimly indeed. He looked at him across the table in the windowless, comfortless Interrogation Room at Police Headquarters, in the light of the big lamp suspended above. Except for the place where the shorthand writer sat at his own small table, the corners of the room were in shadow. Detective Constable Cassidy stood with his back to the closed, soundproof door.

24

Gerry did not like being in the "grillroom" and his expression showed it. But his jaw was set in an equally obvious resolve to say nothing which might lead to a charge against himself.

It was Martineau's intention that Gerry should like the place of inquisition even less as time went by, and he started the process of discomfiture with a leisurely inspection of the contents of the man's pockets. These were lying on the table.

He picked up a notecase, and when he saw that it was packed with five-pound notes he raised his eyebrows and whistled.

"I do a lot of ready-money dealing in my business," said Gerry.

Martineau nodded impassively. He put the notecase down without bothering to count the money, and picked up a wallet. He looked at photographs, documents, driving license, and put it down. Nothing else interested him except a heavy gold cigarette case.

"Gold is an investment," Gerry said.

Again Martineau nodded. No doubt Gerry had acquired the case after a big win on the horses. A man of his character needed a reserve of that sort, a means of raising money when nobody would lend him any.

"Some people invest in gold," he said. "Others invest in night clubs."

Gerry was silent, and quite still.

"Verney Barton invested in a night club," Martineau went on placidly. "He invested five hundred. Pounds, nicker, jimmy o'goblins. Do you remember that investment?"

Gerry remained silent.

"Answer me," Martineau insisted, though he was still quite calm. "Do you remember or have you forgotten?"

"That's a real copper's question."

"All right, I'll put it another way. Do you remember or don't you?"

"I'm not compelled to answer any questions."

"Ah, so you do remember."

"I *don't* remember."

"Of course you do. How did you induce Verney to part with a large lump of his life's savings?"

Gerry was silent again.

"Was there some unresponsive girl he fancied? Did you promise to pimp the job for him?"

"I'm not a pimp!"

"Look, it's no use your wriggling. You're on the hook. I don't know *why* Verney parted with his money, but the rest of it is an open book to me. I've seen the document you gave him in exchange for the money. Several other police officers saw it too. We made copies of it."

"You mean you made up copies, in collusion."

Martineau smiled. "We photographed it, too."

There was a long silence. The chief inspector lit a cigarette while he waited.

"All right," said Gerry eventually. "Verney did make an investment in the club."

"I've already told you that. Tell me something I don't know."

"It was a good investment."

"Ah. Happen I didn't know that."

"There was nothing wrong with it."

"So Verney's estate still owns a share of the club."

"No," said Gerry, after a slight pause. "I paid him out."

"When?"

"Sunday. Last Sunday morning."

"That was the morning after the night Verney was reported missing."

"Yes, but I didn't know he was missing."

"Where did you see him?"

"At the club. I'd gone down there to do one or two bits of jobs. He walked in and asked me to pay him out, in cash. Sunday morning, mind you. I managed to scrape up four hundred. I gave him that and owed him a hundred, and he gave me the contract back."

"What did you do with it?"

"I put a match to it. It was done with."

"What time was this?"

"Just before noon."

"Ah. How was Verney, by the way?"

"All right. A bit agitated."

"Was he very pale?"

"Come to think of it, he was a bit pale."

"Didn't he say he was feeling poorly?"

"No."

"No bandage on his head?"

"Bandage? No."

"Are you sure?"

"No, I'm not sure. He kept his hat on."

"A man can't usually wear his hat over a bandage."

"All right then, no bandage."

"Were you alone when Verney came?"

"Yes. Nobody else was in the club."

"You left the front door open and went through to your office, with all that liquor in the bar? Cigarettes too."

"I went in the back way. I could have heard anybody trying to pass the office. I heard Verney. He came the back way."

"You're a good ad-libber, Gerry, but your audience isn't responsive."

"That's the truth, and you can't shake it."

"I'll shake it till it falls to pieces, and you with it. If Verney was alive that Sunday morning he was very ill. He wasn't fit to walk up any steps or make any sort of deal."

"How do you know that?"

"I have evidence. And I know that Verney could not have got that contract after I replaced it in his shoe. The only way you could have got it was by stealing it or getting somebody to steal it for you. That little job was done on Sunday morning. You did it, or had it done, because you knew Verney was dead."

Gerry must have thought he was getting through the interrogation quite well. And he must have felt perfectly safe in the new matter which had arisen. His answer was bold. "Oh, so it's got to murder now, has it?"

"As far as I'm concerned it's been murder for a long time. But I didn't mention it. You did."

"It's been in all the papers."

"No mention of murder, but we won't labor the point. What were you doing on Saturday night?"

"I was at the club from eight at night till three in the morning. I can get a dozen people to alibi me."

"That's what I expected. It doesn't put you entirely in the clear, though. Where did you go after three?"

"Home, to bed."

Gerry had no home, really. He lived in lodgings in a run-down part of the city where there were many boardinghouses and furnished rooms. His wife had divorced him years before. Since that separation he had had a number of "wives" and many changes of address.

"Have you got a regular bedmate at the moment?" Martineau asked.

"No," Gerry replied. He did not seem to resent the question.

"What about that good-looking dancer you've got?"

"She works for me, that's all. Anything you've heard to the contrary is all lies."

"Ah. Where does she live?"

"You'd better ask her. She doesn't live with me."

"Happen she has more sense. The four hundred pounds' story is a nice subtle touch. It rings true, except that it isn't. You must have at least two hundred pounds in this notecase."

"Two hundred and fifty-five," said Cassidy, from the door.

Gerry snorted. "I pretended I had only four hundred. That's business. Something you know nothing about."

"That way of doing business I know a lot about. Did he tell you why he wanted the money so urgently?"

"He said he'd been betting, and he was going to get his head beaten in if he didn't pay up."

"That answer is almost a stroke of genius, Gerry. But you can't lay this at the door of some innocent bookie. Verney still had plenty in the bank."

"He might have needed that as well."

"He never drew it out."

Gerry shrugged.

There was an interruption. Martineau was wanted on the telephone.

He was not surprised. He had men searching the Gee Gee Club, and questioning its members and staff. There were men at Gerry's lodgings in Valley Road. There were men making inquiries in the vicinity of the Barton residence. Also, there had been a general call for information about Gerry, and throughout the city detectives were in contact with informants of all types, ready to listen to any whisper of the man's name. The police wanted to know anything and everything about him, or about anybody who might know him.

Martineau excused himself politely, and went to take the call in his own office. The caller was Detective Constable Murray, one of the men who had been searching Gerry's lodgings. "There's nothing here, sir," he said. "But I think I've got a good witness."

"For Sunday morning?"

"Yes, sir. Nobody remembers Gee coming home from the club in the small hours, because they're so used to him coming home at that time. But somebody saw him go out later."

"What time?"

"He was up and leaving the house by half past eight. The landlady's daughter saw him leave. It was so unusual for him to be out of bed at that time she even remembers what he was wearing. It was a tweed suit. A greenish tweed."

"She quite firm about it? A good witness?"

"Yes. Her mother looked like thunder when she came out with it, but I gather from the way she refers to Gee she wouldn't cry if he dropped dead. Anyway, I got her signed statement."

"Good. Has Sergeant Bird sent that suit to the laboratory with Gee's other stuff?"

"Yes, sir. And all his shoes."

"Is the sergeant there now?"

"No, sir. He got a lot of fingerprints from Gee's room, and went back to Headquarters."

"All right. When you've finished there, find out where Gee garages his car, and go there to see what you can get to know about Sunday morning."

"Very good, sir," Murray said, and that was the end of the talk.

Martineau looked at his watch. It was twenty-five minutes past nine, and on the half hour there would be another call. He waited.

The call came, from Detective Constable Hearn in a public telephone kiosk near Verney Barton's home. "There's a little something here, sir," Hearn reported. "Three people saw a man hanging about within view of the Barton place between nine and ten Sunday morning. They're all women who saw him from their own windows, and they were all interested enough to take a real good look at him. Every one of them describes him as tall, good-looking, dark hair, no hat, greenish tweed suit. I thought happen we could put him up for identification."

"Happen we can. Ten o'clock in the morning. See that those witnesses are here. You've done well, but carry on. I want something about his car if you can get it."

Martineau put down the receiver and sat in thought. The information had not been unexpected. There are so few people about in the streets of any British town at nine o'clock of a Sunday morning that no person could hope to move on foot about a neighborhood such as the Bartons' without being noticed, or leave his car for a time without arousing curiosity and conjecture.

It certainly did look as if Gerry Gee had himself broken into the Barton house, and it looked as if he had been alone. If that were the case, there would be iron filings adhering to his tweed suit, and to a pair of his gloves, and to a pair of his shoes. Lovely unanswerable material evidence.

The chief inspector spoke to Sergeant Bird on the internal line. "What about dabs?" he asked.

"In Gee's room, one sort only, which must be his. In his office at the club, quite a number of different ones. Besides Gee's, there is one which I have identified."

"Whose?"

"Long Cue Lancaster's."

"That maniac? Gee wouldn't have any dealings with him!"

"Well, he's been in his office."

"All right. Now what about the prints on Barton's shoe?"

"They agree in classification with Gee's first and second fingers, left hand. There are also a number of individual characteristics in agreement."

"Enough to swear to?"

"I think so. I'll know for certain when I've blown them up. He took his gloves off, all right, and he was sweating plenty. He must have got excited when he found what he was looking for."

"Yes, it makes them careless," said Martineau with satisfaction.

After that call he sat awhile, considering Gerry and what could be done with him. At the moment it seemed as if it would be a waste of time to question him further. He was not yet in the right mood to be broken down. Well, a night in the cells might soften him.

Martineau returned to the Interrogation Room. "All right, Gerry," he said, without resuming his seat at the table. "I'm a busy man tonight, so I'll postpone our talk."

Gerry grinned. He started to pick up his property from the table and return it to his pockets.

"You won't need those just yet awhile," the policeman went on crisply. "You're going to be charged and put in a cell until morning."

Gerry was astounded. "You're going to lock me up? You're crazy. You've got no evidence."

"Tomorrow," Martineau promised, "you'll find I have enough evidence to sink you without trace."

FIVE

By HALF PAST ten that night all C.I.D. men were in at Headquarters, with their reports and statements. They had had a hard day, and they would have another hard day on the morrow. Martineau sent them home, keeping a few Evening Duty men on standby. Though the general public did not know it, there was not one prowling detective in the heart of a city of a million people.

At eleven o'clock Martineau also called it a day. He went out to his car, which was standing in the police station yard. His was the last car in the yard. The place was deserted, and the smell of automobiles and their gases had been dispersed. The night air was cool. He breathed deeply, and looked up appreciatively at the black, starry sky. He had a hand on the door of the car when a small sound made him still.

The sound came again. It was like the hiss of a snake. It came from the darkest spot in the yard, in the shadow of a gatepost. Martineau moved in that direction, and discerned a small figure standing there. He knew who it was. Pot Eye Walker had been his faithful informer for many years. He had a sort of affection for the man.

"Hello," he said, mentioning no names and keeping his voice pitched low.

"Coo, I thought you was never comin'," the old rogue whispered fretfully. "I've hung about here till me feet's like ice."

"Why didn't you phone?"

"I don't like phone boxes when they're lit up at night. Folk can see you an' start wonderin'. They know damn well you're not talkin' to a bookie."

Martineau reflected that the precaution had been a wise one. Pot Eye survived as an informer only by being above suspicion. The vaguest rumor that he was a copper's nark would close up all his sources of information, and if the rumor was strong there might be bodily harm to him.

"I don't blame you," the policeman said. "What's bothering you?"

"I heard you pulled Gerry Gee in."

"That's right."

"Has it any connection wi' Northern Steel?"

"I can't say."

That was enough for Pot Eye. "I've been waitin' for a move," he said. "Summat involvin' one o' them fellers."

"What fellows?"

"The fellers I saw wi' Gerry Gee."

"Ah. When was this?"

"Not so fast. This is good, I think."

"Well, there's been no mention of a reward yet. But I dare say Northern Steel would be suitably grateful if your information led to anything."

The informer shuddered audibly. "No. No fear. I don't want my name on no check. These fellers is bad. I want some cash now, an' no more to it. You're the only one I'd trust."

"I couldn't get you more than a fiver from the account."

"Have you that much on you?"

"Yes."

"I'll take it."

Martineau parted with five pounds. If Pot Eye said his information was worth so much, then it would be. But he said, "It'll have to be good."

"I think it is," said Pot Eye. He looked around, though he must have known that there was no other person within hearing of the whispered conversation. "I saw Gerry havin' a bit of a meetin' wi' three more blokes, just two days prior to the Northern Steel job."

"At the club?"

"No. That's what made me start snoopin'. It was eleven o'clock in the mornin' an' I saw Ernie Rapp go into Arturo's Caff. Ernie's always worth a thought, an' I thought he'd gone in there for his breakfuss. Well, I'm goin' on my way an' I sees Long Cue Lancaster walkin', which generally means he's left his car somewhere outa sight. So I turned back, an' behold Long Cue goes into Arturo's. It's not Long Cue's sort of place at all, even when he's hard up. So I thought, 'Oho, there's summat up,' an' I chanced me arm an' popped in for a box of matches."

"Arturo saw you, then?"

"No. Me luck was in. His missus was back of the counter an' she don't know me. He was nowhere in sight. There were only four kids in there, drinkin' Cokes an' stuff. There's no back door, so Rapp an' Gerry could only a-been in that little booth at the back, where there's one table an' room for five or six to sit. I mean, they must a-been together, see?"

"Yes. And Arturo with them, perhaps?"

"Happen so. Well, I cleared out of there as soon as I'd got me matches, an' I nipped into that baker's an' confectioner's across the street. They have a mornin' coffee place upstairs, an' it were full of women an' insurance men. You never heard such a clack. Lucky it isn't one of them posh places, an' I'd had a shave as it happened. There were just one empty chair at a winder table, an' I took it. Three women at the table looked at me as if I were bad fish, an' stopped their gabbin'. Happen they couldn't do wi' me listenin', 'cause they supped their coffee and cleared off.

"I sat there with a cupper coffee an' saw Rapp come out of Arturo's. Then I saw Long Cue Lancaster. Then a feller I don't know, blowin' his nose all the time. He hopped on to a bus at the stop. So I waited an' saw Gerry Gee come out an' walk off. I waited another quarter of an hour, but I didn't see nobody else."

"Can you describe the man who had his handkerchief to his face?"

"Yes. Medium height, medium build. Middlin' strong, I'd say. Dressed very ordinary. Dark-gray suit, dirty shoes nearer gray nor black, floppy gray trilby. I couldn't tell you his age, but he didn't walk like an old man."

"Like a young man?"

"He could a-been young, or he could a-been forty or forty-five. It's hard to tell. If he was older, he was fit. No belly on him."

"And that's the lot?"

"That's all I saw. Happen there could a-been one or two more."

"Thanks. I'll just see if the coast is clear."

Martineau looked out of the yard and peered around. There was nobody in sight and no sign of movement. He gave the word, and Pot Eye emerged and slipped away with his danger-ously earned fiver in his pocket.

Martineau returned to his office pondering. The mention of Long Cue Lancaster had been in accord with previous infor-mation. He was bad; in fact, he was a shocker. A man utterly reckless and utterly unscrupulous, with a record long and bad. Among other penalties, he had been deprived for life of his driving license for an act of manslaughter which some witnesses had declared to be deliberate murder. Yes, he was bad. But Ernie Rapp! Five feet two inches of concentrated venom. Tough, bitter, fearless, pitiless, most evil. A man who went into violent action at the slightest provocation—often, indeed, without provo-cation—and afterwards tried to avoid the consequences though he was never in dread of them. He was a man who had always been a lone wolf because no one would accept him as accomplice or friend. Until now. What on earth had ever induced even an unrighteous fellow like Gerry Gee to sit in conference with such a murderous little bastard? Where was the gang leader who was going to keep Ernie Rapp in order?

Martineau sighed as he sent for records. "Somebody is going to get hurt before this job is over," he decided.

While he waited he thought about Arturo, whose real name was Arthur Beckett. Arturo was a heavy-set Cockney who looked as if he had come from Spain or Italy. He had never been nearer than Brighton to either country, but he liked to amuse his customers by speaking broken English. So far as the Granchester police were concerned, he had simply arrived in the town about five years ago and opened a snack bar. He had drawn the attention of the authorities to himself by applying for a wine license, which had not been granted. He had come to Martineau's notice through one incident. One Saturday night, gibbering with rage, he had picked up a meat knife and attacked a cheeky youngster in his own bar. The youngster had escaped with a cut hand and Arturo with a fine. Martineau resolved to find out what the London Police District knew about him.

With regard to the man who had held his handkerchief to his face, Martineau reflected that he could not have been Verney Barton. Verney had been small and spare, and nobody had ever suggested that he looked even "middling" strong. There was nothing against Verney yet. He was emerging whiter and whiter as the investigation went on.

So there were Long Cue Lancaster, Ernie Rapp, Gerry Gee, and the handkerchief man. Martineau wanted at least two more active helpers in the Northern Steel job. Arturo? Quite likely. Jud Wragg, bouncer at the Gee Gee Club? Possible, certainly. He shook his head. There was another man as yet completely unknown. He felt sure of it. Gee had a certain facile intelligence. He might be the brains of the gang, but he was not strong enough to be the leader. The nose blower or the unknown sixth man would be the leader.

The records of Lancaster and Rapp were put before Martineau. Both had been taken from the Special Section, a part of C.R.O. built up by Chief Superintendent Clay. Special Section records contained a brief biography and character sketch of each subject. They were "off the record" records designed to help officers who contemplated arrest or interrogation.

Martineau noted with surprise that Long Cue's father had been a Methodist minister. "Probably died of a broken heart," he mused. Long Cue would have had a good education if he had not been expelled from every school he attended, until he arrived at one in which detention and not expulsion was the rule. That place had been one of H.M. Approved Schools, full of bad boys like himself. The theft of a motorcar, at the age of fourteen, had taken him there. His occupation was now given as motor engineer, and it was stated that he was a gifted mechanic and an outstanding driver. Except for a trifling offense of rape, which had earned him three years in Leeds Prison, all his crimes had been connected with motor vehicles. He was six feet six inches tall, slim in proportion to his height, but wiry and strong. Those six and a half feet would make him too noticeable to be one of the attackers in the Northern Steel robbery. If he took part in that crime, Long Cue had been a wheel man, and probably the head wheel man.

At least Long Cue had had a chance in life. That appeared to have been denied to Ernie Rapp. Now twenty-eight years of age, he was the son of an unmarried woman who was still the prey of any man who wanted her. Rapp had been a thief since he could walk, almost. He had taken the bread from the hands of his even more unfortunate brothers and sisters. Reaching up to steal from the counters of walk-around stores, he had become a known thief before he reached the age of criminal responsibility. Before he reached that age he blinded a playmate with a razor belonging to a man who was currently living with his mother. He had learned to be a criminal in every sort of remand home, approved school, Borstal institution, and prison. Theft and violence was his record. He had been birched and he had been flogged, and such punishment had left him quite indomitable. There was no sex crime on his record. With regard to sex he appeared to be normal, though entirely amoral and absolutely without chivalry.

Everybody knew that Ernie was a rat, and everybody knew that Ernie would never make a noise like a rat, or a pigeon, or a canary. Ernie would never squeal, nor would he sing. It was his habit to tell the police nothing, ever, about anything.

Long Cue Lancaster had a similar reputation.

And there Martineau thought he saw at least one reason why those two men could be involved with Gerry Gee. They were known to be trustworthy in one respect.

For Martineau, in Gee's place, that would not have been enough. Those two men were not only intractable, they were also unpredictable. With them the impulse was invariably followed

37

by the deed. Even with a share of £29,000 at stake, neither man would be able to change his nature.

Before he did finally go home to bed, Martineau decided that Long Cue and Rapp should each have a can tied to his tail. He made arrangements for those two to be located and kept under surreptitious observation for twenty-four hours a day. It would mean taking many of his best officers from other duties, but, if they could follow without being spotted, it might be worth while. Thieves with money put away are apt to be overcome with the desire to know if it is still safe in its hiding place. Either Long Cue or Rapp, or both, might want to take a look.

If they could be followed without seeing that they were followed—that was the snag. Martineau had one or two men who were really good at the tailing game. He did not have a dozen.

SIX

THE OTHER SIDE

ARTURO'S CAFÉ was a third-rate snack bar in a second-rate main street. But when Ben entered the place he was not offended by the smell because his mind was too fully occupied with other matters. He looked at four youths sitting at a table, and decided that their presence was of no consequence. He went to the counter, and met the hard, level glance of the man standing behind it. This one, a swarthy, heavy-set fellow, did not speak but lazily made an inclination of the head toward the rear of the premises. Ben took the hint, and went on. In a roomy rear booth, at a table with a clean, newly laid cloth, he found Gerry Gee.

"Ah, good lad, Ben," said Gerry, rising and offering his hand. "You've made it."

"Yes," Ben replied. "But I'm not joining in this thing."

"Don't say that," Gerry said easily. "Sit down and we'll talk about it. I'll get you some coffee."

Ben sat down. Gerry rapped on the table with a spoon. The swarthy man brought coffee. When he had gone, Gerry offered cigarettes and said, "Arturo's all right. He's one of us."

"I don't want to know," Ben told him.

39

"Ah, but you do know now. You've got to know. The whole idea was yours in the first place."

"I only happened to mention it. I wasn't serious."

"You seemed serious enough to me."

"You could see I wasn't. I don't go in for that sort of thing."

"Neither do I, as a rule. But as you so kindly pointed out at the start, this is a piece of cake. It can't go wrong."

"All right, get on with it. *I* won't say anything."

"You might. We've got to be sure. That's why you're in."

Ben sighed, with exasperation. Seemingly a man couldn't open his mouth to some folk. All this had started from a simple comment. During the negotiation of a perfectly legal job of work, Ben had suggested an advance to cover the cost of materials. With good humor Gee had replied that he wanted credit, that his name was Gee, not Gerard. Lord Gerard of the Northern Steel Corporation was undoubtedly the richest man for many thickly populated miles around. Ben had remarked that Lord Gerard was due to be relieved of some of his wealth. During his own legitimate visits to his bank he had observed that the men who collected the Northern Steel payroll were vulnerable. He had told Gee about this, simply as a matter of ordinary gossip. It was just his luck that he had gossiped with a man of this sort. Now he was here, being roped into a robbery.

"Who's going to make me be in it?" he growled.

"Steady. We're all friends here," Gerry replied with a smile. He rapped the table again, and when Arturo appeared he asked, "Anybody come yet?"

"Lew."

"Ask him to come back here."

Arturo went away, and another man appeared. He was a big broad man with a firm, blunt-featured face, a dark complexion, dark hair, and uncommonly light gray eyes. He wore a pearl-gray felt hat at a raffish angle, his light suit was well pressed, his shirt immaculate, and his brown shoes highly polished. None of this elegance could hide his inbred vulgarity. He could never have been a gentleman under any definition of the term.

He leaned against the end of the partition with an unlit cigarette in his mouth, negligently tossing and catching a gold-colored Colibri lighter. He and Ben eyed each other. Ben was a

40

strong young man, and a reasonably brave one, but this cavalier of the back streets daunted him. The strongest of his instincts told him that here was a person violent, cruel and implacable; the sort of man whose presence made his cronies uneasy and his prospective victims acutely unhappy.

"Lew Cory," said Gerry. "Clean and clever. Always dressed to kill."

Cory's thick, firm lips parted to show excellent teeth. He did not offer his hand, but continued to hold Ben's gaze. "So this is the lad," he said. "Is he in?"

"Not yet."

Cory sat down at the table. He lit his cigarette, inhaled deeply, and spoke through the smoke. "He will be," he said, stating a fact. "We need him."

"He don't see it our way, yet."

"He will."

It was a real effort for Ben to refute the confident monosyllables. "You can't make me," he said.

"Words, words," said Cory, not impatiently. "Why argue? You got to come in because we need to be sure of you, an' because you're the only one who can hide the take for us. You're respectable, the cops won't even think of you. They might chase some of us around, but we'll be clean. We won't talk, you can be sure of that. You'll be able to hold the cash till it's safe to have the divvy."

"Gerry here could hide the money."

"Him? I'd never sleep a wink if he had it."

Gerry laughed. "That's about it, Ben. We can trust each other not to come copper, but we can't trust each other with money. You're the only one we can trust."

"Why?"

"Because your stake here is too big to be left behind. You're a partner in a good business, and you'll have the whole of it when your old man dies. And you'll have his money. You're not going to run away and leave all that behind."

Ben was silent.

"That don't mean you can't do with an extra few thousand, free of tax," Gerry went on. "Nobody can have too much."

"The risk isn't worth it for me."

"Risk? What risk? It'll be a lovely tickle. And with you holding the proceeds there'll be no risk at all. We'll all be wearing
masks. None of us will be recognized and whatever happens
none of us will ever cough for the coppers. You can be sure of
that. That's the one qualification we've all got. We'll have seven
or eight thousand apiece for a couple of hours' work."

Ben thought about that. He could buy a better car than the
one he had. He had always fancied a really high-class sports car.

"How do we share?" he asked.

"All equal shares. This lot won't stand for anything less."

"How many of us?"

"Six, counting you."

"Who are the others?"

"They'll be here in a minute."

Arturo must have been listening. His head appeared at the
end of the partition. "They're here now," he said.

"Send 'em in," Cory said. "Let's get this settled."

Ben did not want to see them. Discretion urged him to get out
of this thing, here and now. He was aware of a heaviness of the
heart when he thought of all the anxiety and risk. He, a man
with a prosperous future assured. It was madness.

But these men expected him to join them, and they had every
intention of persuading or compelling him. He was just the man
they wanted. And it was true that he had been the first to mention the project. He ought to have kept his big mouth shut.

Was there still time to back out? He looked at the two men
who appeared, and the weight on his heart increased. He knew
one of them by sight and reputation. Long Cue Lancaster was
a one-time stock car driver now barred from every track in the
country. A killer on wheels. Six feet six inches of animated
steering column. His loose, bitter face still showed the courage
which remained when all the rest was decadence. He flung himself into a seat at the table, nodded in acknowledgment of Ben's
name, and thereafter watched him with a brooding air.

The other man was small and compact. He was introduced as
Ernie Rapp. He was pale, with hollow cheeks. His clothes were
nondescript. A slum product, Ben thought contemptuously;
undersized, underbred, underfed. When he looked directly at
Ben, the young man saw that his eyes had the shallow glare of

a tormented wild animal's. Worse and worse, he thought.

Arturo came and joined them, and the booth was full, with Ben trapped in a corner. "So we're team-handed," Gerry said with satisfaction. "And we all know what to do, except Ben here."

"What happens if I say I'm not coming in with you?" Ben asked rather desperately.

Nobody answered. They looked at him. He looked at Cory, at Long Cue, and at Rapp. He saw himself lying slashed and beaten in an alley. Lying dead perhaps, if this crew were determined to carry out their project. He saw his father being beaten, as a lesson to his son. He saw his place of business in flames, and in flames again after it had been restored.

"All right," he said. "I'm in."

Cory smiled at him, and reached to grasp his wrist on the table. "That's my boy," he said.

When Ben departed from that place he was apparently blowing his nose, and he kept his handkerchief to his face for some time. He was glad that he was wearing his shabbiest suit and shoes. From now on he had to take precautions.

But he was beginning to feel a little better. The optimism of Gee, Cory and Company was infectious and when it was all over he would be a few thousand pounds in pocket. Then, *never* again.

One thing he had learned from that thieves' conference. He thought he had more brains and imagination than all the rest of them put together. Already his fertile brain had evolved a plan for the safe handling of the loot. But he had kept it to himself, on their advice. They could not trust each other. Only he would know where the money was hidden.

In those circumstances, and with his intelligence, he could not see how any of that mob could cheat him, so he was sure of getting his share.

SEVEN

ON THURSDAY morning Gerry Gee was put in line with nine more men of about the same age, size and type, and he was identified by three women who had seen him loitering in the vicinity of the Barton home on Sunday morning. Also there were two witnesses to the presence of his car in the same district at the same time. And certain steel filings had been extracted by a magnet from the fabric of his tweed suit. These matters, added to the evidence of his fingerprints on Verney Barton's shoe, made a strong case against him.

In court, leaning from the dock, Gerry had a hurried whispered conference with his solicitor. Apparently the fact of his identification had caused a change of plan. The solicitor entered a plea of not guilty, and stated that his client had elected to be tried by jury. It was a shrewd move for several reasons, and the most important of these was that if Martineau had a good case Gerry would be remanded to the Quarter Sessions anyway, and it would be a disadvantage to go before a jury when he had already been found guilty in a lower court. Also, by choosing to go for trial, Gerry had a reasonable chance of being remanded on bail.

The police were in disagreement about bail. Clay believed

that Gerry would be more useful at large, under observation. Martineau wanted him in prison, where he could be kept in ignorance of events and interrogated regularly about the Northern Steel job. Clay was the boss. He put up an effective smoke screen by opposing bail, but he had already told the magistrate's clerk that he wanted Gerry out and about. Gerry was remanded on bail, on his own recognizances, until the Quarter Sessions. Martineau's frown showed his displeasure.

Soon after Gerry's release, Clay was able to say, "I told you so." At twelve noon the club owner was seen to make two brief but agitated telephone calls from a public kiosk. At the exact time of the first call, Long Cue Lancaster was observed waiting near a kiosk. The phone in the kiosk began to ring, and he entered the box and answered the call. At the time of the second call another observer saw Ernie Rapp answer the ring from yet another kiosk. Immediately afterwards Long Cue was observed to make two calls, and Rapp made one. These happenings strengthened Martineau's opinion that the gang he pursued had no more than six members. They also went some way toward proving that Pot Eye Walker had been telling the truth.

Bearing in mind that the unknown members of the Northern Steel gang might also be members of the Gee Gee Club, Martineau decided to put a man in there. With violent characters like Lancaster and Rapp in the offing, he realized that his undercover agent ought to be a man who was big enough to look after himself, and he thought of P. C. Ainslie's impressive physique. Ainslie would do. He was from an outer division and likely to go unrecognized.

So, that Thursday night, Joe arrived at the club with a story about having had the place recommended to him. He was, he said, temporarily employed in the town as a construction engineer. Normally, his size would have made him suspect, and the staff of the club were usually very alert for signs of police infiltration, but this was the day *after* the raid. They did not expect to be bothered again by the police for quite some time. Joe paid a fee of one guinea, and became a country member.

The club was in a well-chosen spot, in a little yard in a commercial district in the heart of the city. The streets were thronged in the daytime, but at night they were almost deserted, so that people visiting the club could park their cars without trouble. The neighborhood also had another advantage from a club owner's point of view: there were no residents to complain about noises made late at night by departing members.

The police were inclined to look at all clubs with unfriendly eyes, but they had been compelled to admit that the Gee Gee was well run. None but members were admitted, on the principle that if a man could not afford a guinea he was a waste of time to everybody, including himself. There were many pretty hostesses, and their wages were nominal. They were required to behave decorously while they were on the premises, and at least discreetly after closing hours. Gerry Gee enforced the requirement in a very simple way. He had a rule that no person with a police record could be employed at the club. If one of his girls was careless enough to be caught in a legally immoral act after she had left the club, she was barred from entering again. If the girl's offense was more serious, the consequences for her could also be more serious. There was a case of a girl who tried to blackmail one of the more wealthy members after he had stayed with her in her flat for the best part of a night. Subsequently an unknown person marked her for life, with a razor. Every member of the club's staff had an alibi on that occasion.

Gerry himself liked to say that he was strict with the girls. He could afford to be strict, because he had a waiting list. Girls were ten a penny.

The club had many members who could be described as respectable, but Gerry's rule about police records did not apply to them. Inevitably some members were of a shady sort while a few were criminals of a presentable type. Members were of course allowed to bring their wives into the club, but it was significant that few of them ever did. One does not ship oil to Texas or coal to Newcastle. There were always lots of girls.

Having been briefed about the foregoing matters, Joe was agreeably surprised by the atmosphere and décor of the club itself. He understood that it had once been a tea merchant's warehouse. Now there were curtains of golden velvet, and much white paint. The long bar was a glitter of bright light, mirrors and polished glass. On the walls were horse's head murals, not badly executed. There were round tables of different sizes around a small dance floor. A small band of musicians made pleasant noises without making a nuisance of themselves.

Joe carefully avoided catching the eye of any of the hostesses as he wanted time to look around. The first floor show was about to begin, and there were about twenty members present. Joe sat at a small table close to the wall. He paid a large price for a small gin and settled down to watch the show. The compère was a sophisticated comedian who cracked bawdy jokes and introduced a close harmony group of three girls, a pair of professional ballroom dancers, and a young woman who sang off-key in an excruciating manner which he described as "technique." Joe was not impressed. All this was local talent. He hoped that the star of the show would be better; this dancer they called Cleo Patra.

When she appeared, the dancer wore a modified ballet dress, glittering and colorful, and a tiny, slant-eyed, glittering mask. Joe was stirred by the way she moved. He thought that her figure was splendid and he was fascinated by her legs, and by her glorious coppery hair. Maybe she was not Pavlova, but she was lovely.

Applause for the dancer brought an encore, this time with the support of the masculine half of the ballroom team.

After the floor show the band played dance music. A few couples danced. Then Cleo Patra reappeared. She was wearing a dress which was not markedly different from other dresses being worn in the room, but to her newest admirer she was as outstanding as a brilliant-cut diamond in a parcel of rough. Her face was as he had imagined it, a lovely face which looked as if it could change according to her mood. Her eyes were a light, hot brown, almost the color of topaz. The face and eyes promised character and courage. Joe wondered if the promise was a lie. He supposed he would never know. "She's not for the likes of me," he decided.

But as the girl crossed the room she looked once at Joe, directly at him and at no one else. Then she went to a table where

47

an elderly man was sitting alone. The man rose, and greeted her as if he knew her well. But he was respectful too, and obviously pleased to have her at his table.

She had only been seated at the table a minute or two when a youngish man approached her and asked her to dance. She refused, but with a smile. It occurred to Joe that Gerry Gee might expect her to mix with the customers between shows. But even so it seemed that she could choose with whom she would associate.

Then the girl looked at Joe again, not in invitation but with the directness which had been in her first glance. His interpretation of that look filled him with dismay. She had seen him somewhere and she knew him for a policeman, he felt sure. He assumed that quite soon she would go behind the scenes and inform her employer that there was a police spy on the premises. Then he would be asked to leave, or at any rate he would not be allowed to see any incident worth a report.

The girl had looked away, but now she was looking at Joe again. He ventured to smile. She also smiled, and looked away.

The dance ended. Another started. A plump, middle-aged man—an excellent dancer, as Joe had seen—went to Cleo Patra and asked her to dance. Smiling, she declined. Almost immediately afterwards her glance strayed in Joe's direction. Perhaps then she decided that she was behaving indiscreetly. She began to pay more attention to the remarks of her table companion.

Joe remembered that he was on duty. He reflected on what would happen if he reported to Martineau that he had seen the girl who was his ideal of loveliness. Well, there had been little else to report.

He looked around. Now there was a big man in evening dress standing near the curtain which led to the rear. His huge neck and big, black-jowled face made the tiny bow of his black tie look ridiculous. Joe guessed that he would be Jud Wragg, the club's undermanager and bouncer. Martineau had said that he was doubtful about Wragg. He was a man to be watched.

Gerry Gee appeared beside Wragg. The two men stood together a little while, smiling and nodding at dancers as they drifted by. Then Gerry skirted the dance floor and began to move among the tables, having a word here and there with the members. He stopped to speak to Cleo Patra's companion. Joe studied her as the men exchanged a few words. She seemed to be listening without interest.

Gerry moved on. He arrived at Joe's table. "Evening," he said with a smile. "New member?"

"That's right. It's a very nice club."

"Glad you like it." Gerry's glance moved to four girls who were sitting at a table not far away. Three of the girls were watching expectantly, waiting for a signal. His smile became something of a leer. "Don't be afraid to avail yourself of the facilities," he said.

"I might get around to that."

"Do, by all means," said Gerry. He passed on. Joe had detected no suspicion behind his affability. Seemingly all was well.

A dance ended, and another began. The band played a sweet, slow little tune. Gerry finished his round of the tables, and disappeared behind the curtain. The girl's glances were again straying in Joe's direction.

He was not much of a dancer, but he could shuffle round the floor to a tune like this. He had seen the girl refuse two requests to dance. She would probably refuse a third, but there could be no harm in asking.

He got up and went over to her. She saw him, and for a moment she seemed to be in a panic. That look of fear almost stopped him. This would be a third refusal, he felt sure. He stood beside her. He was aware of her companion's smile. It was not a proprietary smile, and there was no jealousy in it, but some kindliness and pity. This man also expected Joe to be refused.

The girl's eyes had dropped, and Joe could see the dark lashes. "May I have the pleasure of this dance?" he managed to say. Without a word she rose and took his arm, and they moved on to the dance floor.

With Cleo in his arms, Joe fell into his shuffle. At least his timing was good. The girl had no difficulty in dancing with him, and indeed she made him feel that he was a better dancer than he had thought. He relaxed, and even began to enjoy himself. He looked down at his partner. She looked up, and they smiled at each other. They continued in silence for a while, and then she said, "It took you long enough to make up your mind. I

49

thought I was going to have to get a flag and wave it."

"Well," he said. "For one thing, I can't dance."

She laughed. "It's a fact you can't. But I've seen worse."

"Had you guessed I'd be a poor dancer?"

"Yes. You're just about what I expected."

"You must have expected something pretty bad. I thought you were going to faint when you saw me headed your way."

Again she laughed. "I can't explain that. I just went all dithery when I saw you coming. Goodness knows why. You're no Rock Hudson."

He grinned. He was beginning to get the hang of this girl. He suddenly felt at home with her. "Well," he said complacently, "you didn't refuse me."

"After I'd waited all that time? My goodness, I didn't think you were the hesitating sort."

"I'm not. But I'd seen you refuse two men. Besides, you're the well-known Cleo Patra, and I'm just a steel erector."

"A what?"

She sounded so surprised that he looked down at her face. She was gazing up at him with an expression quite strange. She said, "You weren't a steel erector the last time I saw you."

Dismay silenced him. He was busted. Blown to blazes. She had spotted him right away, and passed on the word somehow, and Gerry Gee had come around to have a look at him. And now she was telling him that he'd been spotted. Surely it would have been better tactics to keep him in ignorance, as Gee had done?

They danced on, but he sensed that she was waiting for an answer. Her remark had been a challenge which he had to take up. Perhaps, he thought, she had not passed the word to Gee after all. Perhaps she was just telling him that she knew he was a policeman, so that he would go away before any harm was done.

"What was I the last time you saw me?" he asked.

"I'd better not say. If you're here incognito, you won't want me to breathe a word, will you?"

"Not if you can afford to keep quiet."

"In this place the tables have ears."

"Does anyone know my, er, secret?"

"I don't know. I haven't said anything."

"That's good of you."

"Don't mention it," she answered dryly.

He said, "Are you disappointed in me, being here under cover?"

"No. I was just thinking that I must be dim, after Gerry's affair. I thought you were having a night out, like everybody else. Evidently I don't know enough about—about men like you."

He was beginning to feel very happy about something. This glorious girl had known that he was a policeman and had been willing to know him as a policeman. He had been socially acceptable to her. That was remarkable. It was wonderful.

"Did you think I came here after the girls?" he asked.

She showed him that she had a dimple. "If you did you've been pretty slow about it. You've been here an hour and a half. Of course, you *are* slow."

He had been there an hour and a half. She knew that. She had observed him from some place as soon as he had entered. She could have blown him as high as Ararat right at the start. "She's all right," he decided. "She's on my side."

The music stopped. He was unwilling to release her. The band leader was looking at her, ready to play an encore. She shook her head.

"Oh, I say," Joe protested.

"Let's not be too obvious at the start."

It was almost as if she were reminding him that he had a job to do. "All right," he said. "But can I have another dance, later?"

"No. Not tonight. I have to do my number."

"Can I see you again?"

"Now he's talking," she said to an invisible third person.

"When?" he asked eagerly. The eagerness was visible. She had to cool his ardor.

"I'm in the phone book. Cleo Patton," she said. "Drop me a line."

"Patton? I'll ring you up."

"Yes, you could do that."

"When will I find you at home?"

He was still much too eager, and people were watching.

51

"You'll have to take your chance on that," she said coolly. "Now go back to your table and don't stride right over anybody on the way."

He grinned and accepted the dismissal. Her words had been timely. He could have started jumping over tables through sheer exuberance.

EIGHT

"THERE doesn't seem to be much in these observations of yours," said Martineau. It was a comment rather than a complaint.

Nevertheless, Joe colored. "There was hardly anything to report, sir."

The senior detective's eyes narrowed. "Who did you speak to? Tell me *everybody* you spoke to."

"Well, there was the man who signed me in and took my subscription as a country member. He just asked me the questions necessary for membership."

"Yes, go on."

"The man Gee came and we had a word at our table, as stated. Then I had a dance with a girl."

"Hmmm. What did she have to say?"

It was no use. Joe dared not withhold it. "She had me spotted, sir. She'd seen me in uniform somewhere. But she hadn't blown me. She hadn't said a word to a soul."

Martineau raised his eyebrows. "Are you sure of that?"

"As sure as I could be in the circumstances. I had to take her word for it. She might have been kidding me, but I don't think so."

53

"Why didn't you put this in your report?"

Joe had nothing to say. Made-up excuses would only have made matters worse.

"Look," said the chief inspector patiently. "Suppose I had wanted to put you in there again? I might have been sending in a man known to be a policeman: known by the entire staff and half the members."

"If you had detailed me to go there again, sir, I would have told you."

Martineau appeared to accept that. He looked up curiously at the young man who stood before him. "Is there something special about the girl?" he wanted to know.

"She's not an ordinary sort of girl."

"Very few of the wenches who work for Gerry Gee are ordinary girls. They're mostly bags. They're very smart luggage, but they're bags just the same. Did you know that?"

"Yes, sir."

"But you don't seem to think that *this* one is a bag. If you're right, which I doubt, she might be of use to us. What's her name?"

"Cleo Patton, sir. She's a professional dancer at the club."

Martineau was completely taken by surprise, but his face did not change. In silence he sat looking at Joe, who met his gaze without wavering. He wondered if he had made a mistake in thinking that this Ainslie was good C.I.D. material. He was an experienced policeman, with six years' service. Could *any* policeman with six years' service really be so naïve?

"I suppose you know that this Cleo Patton has worked at the Gee Gee Club for quite some time," he said reasonably. "She might even have an interest in the place. She is certainly on friendly terms with Gerry Gee, and some people think she's his woman. And you, meeting her for the first time last night, actually believe that she didn't inform the management the moment she spotted you?"

"I suppose it seems idiotic to you, sir, but that's what I believe."

Martineau was somewhat amused. He asked, "Have you made any arrangements with Miss Patton?"

"She said I might telephone her, at her home."

"Mmmm." The chief inspector sat in thought. Finally he said,

"I think we'll play this. It's quite clear that you're smitten with the girl, and I wouldn't say that I altogether blame you for that. She's taken a fancy to you, or else she's kidding you. Either way, you'll have to look out for yourself. She knows you're a copper, so at any rate *you're* not deceiving *her*. Whether or not she's shopped you, you will try to improve your acquaintance with her, and all the time you'll remember that you're a policeman. They can't be on their guard all the time: you might stumble on to something. Anyway, you'll get all the information you can, and you'll report it. All of it. Is that clear?"

"Yes, sir."

"Very well. Now go and get cracking on the phone. And tonight you'll be on plain-clothes duty inside the Gee Gee again."

That interview occurred at half past nine of a crisp, sunny Friday morning. The instruction had been to "get cracking," but Joe decided that a night club dancer would want to sleep until at least eleven o'clock. He had no paper work to do, and it would have done him no good at all to wait, visibly idle, in the C.I.D. So he slipped out of the building and went to a coffee bar.

At twenty minutes to eleven he was back again, making his phone call from one of the soundproof booths in the main office. Cleo answered immediately.

"It's me," he said. "The policeman you met last night."

"I recognize your voice, but I don't know your name."

"It's Ainslie. Joe Ainslie."

"Joe," she said, savoring the name. "Joe is all right. It suits you. You're definitely not a Nigel or an Adrian."

"When can I see you?"

"I don't know. What are you doing?"

"I'm at your disposal all day. I'll be on duty tonight."

"Ah. Have you got a car, or anything?"

"I have an old M.G. Open two-seater."

"This is just the day for an open car. Will you take me somewhere?"

"Sure. Delighted. Seaside or countryside?"

"Country. Anywhere as long as it's nice. I'll pack some sandwiches."

"That won't be necessary. We can have lunch somewhere."

"Sandwiches," she said firmly. "You'll have to learn not to waste your money."

"Why?" he asked foolishly.

She ignored the question. "Where do you garage your car?"

"Near my digs in Shirwell."

"I'll get a bus to Shirwell, and meet you in front of that big cinema on the corner, at half past eleven."

"You mean the Regent? Right, I'll be there."

That was the end of the talk. Joe hurried home to change into his tweed suit, which was also his best suit, and get out his car. He waited ten minutes beside the Regent Cinema. Cleo arrived looking like a million dollars—in his opinion—in a light coat and flat-heeled shoes and a little white cap.

There was no way of motoring out of Granchester without passing through miles of suburbs and satellite towns. Joe headed northeast, for the dales of Yorkshire. They talked. He learned that she was twenty-four years old, the daughter of two variety artists. He told her that he was twenty-seven, the son of a shipwright and himself a shipwright by trade. "I can always go back to it if I don't do any good in the police," he said.

He told her about life in a shipyard, and about life in the police force. Also, she was interested in the towns and villages through which they passed. Some of the time they drove along in silence; a comfortable, friendly silence. A little after one o'clock they were sitting on the grass beside a stream. They could see small trout and grayling in the clear water. Behind them at a little distance was a tiny, beautiful village and around them were green rolling hills. The sun was warm and the grass was dry. Cleo had taken off her coat.

"It's lovely," she said, filling her lungs. "What do you call this place?"

"This is Wharfedale, and the village is Burnsall. That one across there is called Appletreewick. You get a lot of people here at weekends."

"But now there's just the two of us," she said.

She lay down on her back. He stretched himself out beside her, and they looked up at a solitary white cloud galleon, becalmed in a blue sky. Their hands touched, and the contact was electric. He raised himself on one elbow and looked down into her face. She turned away and sat up quickly.

"I'm hungry," she said. "It's time we had lunch."

They ate the sandwiches and drank the two bottles of beer which he had purchased at the Red Lion Inn on the village green. "Lovely picnic," he commented.

He reflected upon the marvel of himself, a common copper, being here at the riverside with this beautiful and talented girl. "It's funny about us," he said. "I mean, you letting a fellow like me take you out."

"What's funny about it?"

"Well, as soon as I set eyes on you I knew you were just the girl for me. But I never thought I'd ever even get to speak to you."

"Faint heart."

"Nonsense. You seemed to be right out of my reach. But when I did get to you, after a minute or two it seemed as if we'd known each other for ages."

"Well, I have known you for ages, in a way. Months, at any rate. I've seen you here and there, walking about in your uniform. One week, I saw you at the same place every afternoon, directing traffic."

"Will somebody tell me why I didn't see you? How could I miss seeing *you?*"

"I was in a bus."

"Oh," said Joe. There was a brief silence, and then he said, "Have we any future? I'm just a bobby. You're got your career. You wouldn't want to give it up."

She laughed briefly. "Give it up? I've already told Gerry to look for somebody else. I did that a week ago."

He was aghast. "You're moving to London, or some place?"

She shook her head. "You don't understand. I was born in the business. Mum and Dad were not third-rate artists, but they never got anything better than third-rate bookings. We were on the road *all* the time; a week here, a week there. I never had a home, and you can imagine the sort of education I got."

"They educated your feet, at any rate."

"Oh, to be sure. They meant well. Show people always think their kids are going to be great stars. After the dreary struggle

57

they'd had, you'd think my parents would have had other ideas. But they didn't, and I didn't either. Nothing else ever occurred to me. But I used to play with my dolls and pretend I had a home of my own. Even as a child I had a subconscious longing. Now, it isn't subconscious. It's right out in the open."

"You're going to give up dancing?"

"I certainly am."

Her decision made him hopeful. But he felt obliged to voice an objection. "It doesn't seem right. You have the talent and the looks to go right to the top."

"If only you knew the number of times I've had that said to me. By agents who couldn't find me a one-night stand in a workingmen's club. You know what a beating the variety business has taken in the last few years. Well, the artists have taken a beating with it. Perhaps I haven't had the luck I should have had, but anyway it doesn't matter now. I've made other arrangements."

"Haven't you been all right at the Gee Gee Club? Didn't you get a living wage?"

"Oh, yes. And it's been my longest stay anywhere, except London. I was in London, and I did have a bit of luck. Laddie Loder at the Quetzal Club lost a girl called Minty Bossum very suddenly. She was a top attraction but she got mixed up in something and the police took her."

"I remember that case. A big diamond job."

"Yes. Laddie was frantic, and he put me in with a month guaranteed. It was a chance, but it didn't come off. Fellows looking for dancers didn't come to look at me. Except Gerry Gee. At the end of the month Laddie let me go. Gerry made me an offer. It wasn't much, but it was a living. For a time. I made my conditions, and accepted the offer. At least it meant I could settle down in one place for a while."

"Conditions? What conditions?"

"I could see that Gerry had the roving eye. I had to make it clear to him that he wasn't getting a bedmate. He didn't mind. Perhaps he still thought he'd get me anyway. I'll give him his due, he never stops trying."

Joe's face hardened. "Does he bother you?"

"No, not really. I hear a suggestion every time the ghost walks, but that's nothing."

"If he bothers you, just let me know."

"All right, I will. But I think he has enough bother of his own just now."

"He certainly has," Joe agreed, but he did not enlarge on that. Another thought had occurred to him. "At least we can thank the police for you being here with me. If they hadn't made you that opening by removing Minty Bossum . . ."

Cleo smiled. "That's another thing with me. The police thing."

"What do you mean?"

"I spent my childhood in a hundred different towns. Any town which had some sort of theater. I was a stranger everywhere, and I was told that if ever I got lost I must go to the first policeman I saw."

"Nearly every kid is told that."

"Yes, but I was different. I was never on my own ground. I used to look at policemen, from buses or when I was walking on the street. There were kind-looking ones, and some who didn't look kind at all. I used to think that if I got lost I'd go to this or that policeman. Anyway, it started me noticing policemen. Most people never notice them, do they?"

"No. Some people take no more notice of a policeman than of a lamppost. Until something happens."

"So, you see, that's how I came to notice you."

"I hope you thought I was kind-looking."

"No, I didn't. But I'm a sort of expert now, and I thought you were a very fine specimen. It would be a pity if you ever went back to the shipyard."

"I won't. I'll stay on the force just to please you. I'll get promoted, too. Just as long as you stick around."

"Oh, I'll be around. After some trial and error, I've got myself a job."

"You won't need a job if you marry me," Joe said boldly.

"My goodness, and I said he was slow. Steady, young man. You hardly know me."

"I know you enough to marry you, if you'll have me."

"We'll talk about it some other time. I want to prove to myself that I can make a success in business."

"What sort of business?"

"The rag trade. Oh, I've been trying for years, and saving what money I could. First I tried to learn to be a secretary. That didn't go very well. You wouldn't believe what a bad speller I am. Really, I'm *ignorant*. Then I tried modeling, and I found myself in competition with a lot of gilt-edged debutantes who could afford to buy the clothes they were modeling. So it had to be the rag trade. I've always been good at making my own dresses, so I went in for it seriously. I took lessons, lots of lessons. And now I've found a place. An old lady with a little shop in Mere Street, not too far off the beaten track. She has a small clientele of people who won't buy off-the-peg clothes. I'm going in with her so that she can have it a bit easier. The idea is for me to take over gradually. It's all arranged."

"I'm glad. If Gee gets sent to prison, the club might fold up."

"It won't. Tony Young and Jud Wragg can run it without Gerry. Run it better, probably."

"Is Tony Young the man who signs in new members?"

"Yes. He has an interest in the place."

"How many more with an interest in the place?"

Cleo looked surprised. "I don't know. Mr. Olney once told me Gerry had asked him to put some money into the club. He didn't say how much, or whether he had done."

"Olney?"

"Webster Olney, the old gentleman I was sitting with last night. He's a regular attender at the club."

Joe could not resist. "An admirer?"

"A friend. You've no need to be jealous of Mr. Olney."

"Who's jealous?"

"You are, I hope. What would Inspector Martineau say, if he knew?"

Cleo was plaiting three stalks of grass when she asked that question. When no answer was made, she looked at Joe. "Does he know?"

He nodded. "I didn't mention you in my report, but he's a mind reader. He started asking questions. I had to tell him."

"What did he say?"

"He told me to keep on seeing you."

"Is that why you *are* seeing me?"

"No. You know that. Only you could have stopped me from seeing you."

Having said that, he reached for her. She resisted, but not with all her strength. "You're here with me just to please the inspector," she mocked.

He knew a lover's taunt when he heard one. "Shut up," he said, and then his mouth was on hers.

nine

THE OTHER SIDE

By ARRANGEMENT, Ben met Lew Cory in the snug behind the bar of a quiet little inn called the Craven Heifer. He was uneasy. "Are we all right here?" he asked.

Cory was not at all uneasy. "Sure," he replied. "As long as we don't talk so loud. The landlord here wouldn't gobble to a bogey if his fortune an' estates depended on it. What was it you wanted?"

Ben took a deep breath. He stared at his glass of beer, but found no inspiration. There was no easy way of breaking the news. He said, "I'm as worried as hell. My dad found the money."

Cory's control was excellent. He did not even blink. "When was this?" he asked.

"Less than an hour ago. It's a good thing it was time for you to make your call. Otherwise I'd have had to go looking for you."

"The money couldn't have been hid so good if your old man found it."

"It was. It still is. He's the only man in the world who could have spotted it. And then only in certain circumstances. It was the damnedest bad luck."

62

"What does he want? Half of your share?"

"I wish it was only that."

"He won't get more. The boys won't stand for him cuttin' in on theirs."

"He doesn't want any of it. He's more or less heartbroke. He's given me twenty-four hours to return it to the rightful owners."

"An' if you don't?"

Ben shrugged. "He didn't say. I don't think he'd shop me, but he's quite capable of taking the stuff and dumping it somewhere, and then tipping off the police."

"He might be doing that right now."

"No. He'll keep his bargain."

"You're sure?"

"Yes."

Cory pondered, and became a little bitter. "First that damn fool Gee tries to box clever, an' gets the coppers after him, an' now you go an' make a charlie of it. I've been able to keep clear, same as you. Nobody has ever looked my way, an' I haven't had to go near the others. Now I'll have to get hold of one or two of 'em to help me deal with your old man."

"Deal with him?"

"Sure. You'll have to set it up so as we can talk to him. He'll have to be discouraged."

Ben licked his lips. He asked a question, and was afraid of the answer. "How?"

"Oh, we won't hurt him—much. Seein' as he's your old man, we'll be gentle with him. We'll just point out to him how happy an' comfortable an' prosperous he is. An' how happy an' comfortable an' prosperous you are. An' how it'll come to an end for both of you if anythin' happens to that money or if he breathes one single word to anybody."

"You'd do it to me as well?"

"Sure, if you lost the money for us. How do I know you an' your dad aren't cookin' somethin' up between you?"

"I wouldn't do that."

"Words, words. You'd better hide that money somewhere else, just in case. Where is it now?"

"Under—" Ben stopped. He said, "You're not supposed to know. There's no *need* for you to know."

"Well, you'd better move it, for your own sake. Now, how can we fix it to talk to your old man? Somewhere nice an' quiet an' private."

While Ben talked to Cory he experienced the heaviness of heart which had become familiar since his first meeting with the man. Afterwards, on the way home, he dwelt upon the unhappy incident which had led to his father's ultimatum. "I'll give you twenty-four hours." The corny dialogue of real-life melodrama. The old boy might just as easily have said, "Never darken my door again. You are no longer my son." It could come to that. Certainly things would never be the same again. The implicit trust of yesterday was gone forever.

After delivering his ultimatum, the old man had stalked away, shaking off a suppliant, detaining hand. No doubt he had done that because he could no longer hide his grief. At any rate he had not stayed to listen to excuses. Ben had not been able to explain that he had been forced into crime, nor had he been able to give a warning about the murderous natures of the men who had an interest in the stolen money.

Cory was going to do that, with the help of Rapp, or Lancaster. Ben was sickened at the thought of it.

With the feeling of trouble mounting, Ben realized that he had been stampeded by events. He had not had time to think. If only he had been able to follow his father and tell him exactly how things were, the old chap might have been brought to a more reasonable frame of mind. Then had come the important daily signal from Cory. That had been his opportunity to make an appointment with the man. In addition to that, he had been oppressed with the urgency of a certain job of work of which he had been informed just before the meeting with his father. So he had made the appointment with Cory without leaving himself time to follow his father and talk to him. He had told Cory about his father without realizing that he was going too far, too fast.

Now he knew that it was too late to talk to his father. Cory,

Rapp, and Lancaster were now out of his reach until tomorrow. They could not be stopped. The job had been set up. Ben could not stop it now without increasing the distrust and rousing the anger of his accomplices. He dared not do that. They had no restraint when angry. They could ruin everything.

So Ben changed his mind about going home in search of his father. He went back to the works. There was that job to be done. It was an honest piece of business. He was profoundly sorry that he had ever thought of any other kind of activity.

Before leaving the works he telephoned the woman he had expected to meet that night. He told her that he could not see her that weekend. She was obviously disappointed, but she did not demand an explanation. She was like that. One of the best. He resolved to buy her a handsome present when all his troubles were over.

Of course he could have gone to her that night, but he had made up his mind to have another alibi. The woman's home was his alternative hiding place for the Northern Steel money. Not even his father knew who she was or where she lived. Nobody knew. He had always been discreet about that, simply because he would have resented the natural curiosity of friends and relations in a matter which he regarded as the private affair of two people.

In the circumstances there was no obvious reason for him to think that he might require an alibi or for him to expect to be asked about his whereabouts at a certain time. Why, then, was he making preparations? He did not ask himself the question. His mind shied away from it.

TEN

THROUGH Friday and Saturday Martineau's robbery-murder case remained in a condition which he described as "stagnant." The condition was disturbed at 9.15 P.M. on Saturday night when an agitated detective reported that Ernie Rapp had deliberately slipped away from surveillance. He had entered a large and busy public house in a main street, walked straight through it and emerged by the back door, and vanished among the dark alleys behind it. This had been done so quickly that no member of the observation detail had been able to get round the block to the back door in time to see him go.

"Very likely he had his tail spotted ten minutes after we tied it on," Martineau said bitterly to Devery. "Put out the word on him. He must be found, and movements reported. Not to be approached."

At midnight Rapp was still eluding the police. Martineau went home to bed. At nine o'clock on Sunday morning he was back at his desk. There he learned that Rapp had not been seen until he had returned to his home in the poor district of Churlham at three o'clock.

"Six hours," said Martineau wearily. "Now will somebody tell me what he was doing?"

"In a club, with a woman, or doing a job. Or all three," Devery replied promptly.

"Right. Get me Ainslie as soon as he comes in."

It was discovered that Ainslie was already present in the main office. He came at Devery's summons.

"Do you know Ernie Rapp?" Martineau asked.

"No, sir. But I would know him if I saw him. I've seen his picture often enough."

"Was he in the Gee Gee Club last night?"

"Not between nine and two, sir. Unless he was behind the scenes and using the back door."

Martineau nodded. "He could have done that."

He sat in thought. Ainslie remained standing before his desk, awaiting dismissal. The internal-line telephone rang. Absently Martineau picked it up and announced himself.

"Another one for you," said Chief Superintendent Clay.

"Another job?"

"Call it that. Another body at the General Hospital."

"What? In the mortuary?"

"Correct. These days the attendants look in every fridge, every morning. And last thing at night."

"So the body was dumped during the night?"

"It would seem so. Go have a look, will you?"

Martineau was on his feet and reaching for his hat before he had put down the receiver. "Come on," he said, making for the door.

The invitation may only have been meant for Devery, but Ainslie followed and climbed into the back of Martineau's car. When the two senior officers walked into the mortuary, he was with them.

The unidentified body from No. 12 refrigerator had been taken out and put on a slab. On an adjacent slab was the body from No. 4. This had already been recognized as the substitute body by young Dr. Provis. He could not have been wrong. The two stab wounds over the heart were unmistakable signs of murder. It was wearing the shroud and labels of an old man who had died of cerebral hemorrhage the previous day.

"Well, he's a stranger to me," Martineau admitted.

At his elbow, Ainslie said, "They call him Olney. I've seen him in the Gee Gee Club."

"That's it," said the attendant. "I thought I knew the face. He's an undertaker."

"That's right," said Ainslie.

"Or a mortician, as they like to call themselves these days," said Provis, who was quite unperturbed by the discovery of murder. The hospital staff was not really at fault over this one.

"An undertaker," said Martineau thoughtfully. "That sort of hangs together. Undertakers are familiar with morgues, aren't they?"

"They have to come here for bodies," Provis said. "They usually know their way around."

There would have to be an autopsy, but Martineau felt that he could not afford to wait for its findings. He asked, "Off the cuff, would you say these wounds on the chest were the cause of death, doctor?"

"They could be a cause of death," Provis said dryly.

"Have you found any other injuries?"

"Nothing serious. A few bruises which might have been caused by falling from an upright position."

"Thank you." Martineau turned away, for the time being forgetting the body but thinking of its earthly trappings. "We never found Verney Barton's clothes, but we might find Olney's," he said. "And this time we might have a chance of finding something here. Get on the phone and make Bird and Company turn out."

Devery went to execute the order. Martineau said to Ainslie, "Well? Was *he* in the club last night?"

"Yes, sir. He was at his usual table, and Miss Patton sat with him for a while. I had a dance with her and she told me he was in some sort of a mood. She said it wasn't like him to be so quiet."

"Had she any idea as to why he was in a mood?"

"No. I asked her if the old boy was jealous, and she said the idea was ridiculous. We didn't discuss him any more than that."

"Were you in the club when he entered?"

"No, sir. You instructed me not to make myself prominent by going early and staying late every night. I got there at about nine-thirty. He was there at his table, with Miss Patton. I had a dance with her. She went back to him, but at ten o'clock she went to get ready for her number. During the show the big man, Jud Wragg, came and spoke to Olney, who got up and went through the curtain with Wragg. He came back in a minute or two and went toward the front door, as if he were leaving the club. I got the impression he'd been called out by telephone, and I looked at my watch. It was twenty-nine minutes past ten."

"Did he seem perturbed when he went out, as if he'd received bad news?"

"No, sir. I'd say he was more annoyed than perturbed."

"Did you see anything of Gee?"

"Yes. He sat at a table with two men and watched the first floor show right through."

"Was he watching the show when Olney went behind the curtain?"

"Yes, sir, he was."

"Who were the men he was sitting with?"

"I don't know, sir. They were both men in their fifties, both fat and prosperous. They could have been a couple of bookies. After the show I could see them looking round and discussing girls with Gee. When he left them he sent a couple of girls to their table."

"Bloody ponce," Martineau muttered. "All right. Go and see the dancer and see if she can tell you anything else."

"She did tell me something else. After the show she came and sat with me for a little while. I mentioned that Olney seemed to have cleared off, and she said he had knocked on the door of her dressing room and told her he had to go on a job. I asked what sort of a job, and she said, 'Laying out a body.' That's when I found out he was an undertaker. She said he was annoyed at having his Saturday night ruined."

"You seem to have got all you could from her. We can leave her for a while. And we needn't go to the club right away either. As soon as Bird gets here I'm going to Olney's house, and you had better come with me."

While he waited for Sergeant Bird and his men, Martineau discussed the new murder with Devery.

"That phone call was a trick to get Olney away from the club," he said.

"Sure. He was bushwhacked somewhere, done in, and stripped."

"Yes. They'd have to strip him first, somewhere, if they wanted to make a quick switch at the morgue. They'd have to hang about too, until the attendant was called away."

"They had a nerve, trying to work the same gag twice," Devery observed.

"Nerve, or panic, or lack of imagination. They had a body to dispose of and not all the time in the world. No time to make other arrangements. So they tried it again. It had worked once, so why not twice?"

"How do you figure they were short of time?"

"Something had happened quite recently to Olney. He was in a mood. He might have been in a mood to make trouble for somebody, so plans had to be made quickly. Another reason why they were short of time was Ernie Rapp. I think he was in the job. He knew we'd been tailing him, and he knew the word would be out as soon as he slipped his tail. Moving around at night he was taking a chance on being spotted at any time. The longer the time the more chance of being spotted. So it had to be as quick a job as possible."

"Do you think Olney could have been, er, hoist with his own petard?"

"It's an idea, isn't it? After a doctor, an undertaker would be the man most likely to think of the Verney Barton switch. He'd have it in his head already, almost. In his long experience he might have known an actual case where two bodies had been put in the wrong coffins and mourned by the wrong people. Olney *could* have been in the Barton job. I've seen unlikelier crooks. After all, he did spend a lot of time in Gee's club. Those two might have been closer than they seemed."

"We'll have to bear that in mind, sir."

"Yes. Ah, here's Bird and his gang."

Webster Olney had lived in the modest and respectable suburb of Highfield, but only half a mile from the Olney Cabinet Works in bustling Mossbank. To reach Highfield from the hospital, Martineau had to pass through Mossbank, and that being so he decided to take a passing look at the Olney Works.

From his days as a young constable in that area he remembered the Olney Cabinet Works as one of a number of converted stables, with a converted cart shed for a garage. Now, as he approached, he perceived that there had been a complete change. The Olney Works occupied the whole of the ground which had been taken up by a long row of stables and a big stable yard. The old buildings had been demolished, and replaced by a large modern shed and a smaller shed which was evidently the firm's garage. These new buildings shared a concreted enclosure with an open-roofed erection used for seasoning timber, and a stone house which might have been fifty years old. The house had its back to the sheds, and its front door in the next street. It had a well-cared-for look.

"Is that the funeral parlor?" Devery asked.

"Yes, sergeant," Ainslie replied. "The Chapel of Rest."

"Old Dr. Ingham used to live there when I was on the section," Martineau commented.

He would have driven on, but Ainslie said, "The garage door's open."

Martineau stopped the car. He looked. The garage door was not properly closed, though no aperture was visible. He drove the car through an open gateway in the low brick wall which surrounded the premises and stopped beside the garage. The door which had not been quite closed was now opened wider, and a young man appeared.

He was bareheaded, and he had a ruddy, candid face. He had taken off his coat and rolled up his sleeves, but his white shirt was perfectly clean and his gray worsted trousers impeccably creased. He was of medium height and well built, and he looked about thirty years old. He stood, rubbing his hands with cotton waste, and watched the three men alight from the car.

"Morning," he said as they drew near. "What can I do for you?"

Martineau introduced himself, and then he said, "Who are you?"

"My name's Olney. Ben Olney."

71

"Any relation to Webster Olney?"

"I'm his son."

"Oh, yes. About your father—"

"What about my father?"

"I've got bad news for you. Can you take a shock?"

"Yes. Sure. But if you're going to tell me he's been doing something wrong, I don't believe it."

"No, it isn't that. He's dead."

Disbelief was the first reaction. "Dead? Are you sure you haven't made a mistake? You must have. He's at home in bed."

"Are you telling me you've seen him in bed this morning?"

"What? No. I mean, he *should* be in bed."

"Well, I'm afraid he isn't. He's at the General Hospital."

The young man was believing Martineau now. Strain was in his voice, and misery in his face. He said, "I don't understand. When was he taken there? How did he die? What did he die of?"

"He was taken there sometime in the night, after his death. He appears to have died of knife wounds."

"Knife w——? Dad?" The clear eyes were blurred by pain and bewilderment.

Martineau knew what to do in matters of this sort. Don't let them dwell on the bad news. Keep them busy while they're getting used to the idea. He asked, "When did you last see him?"

"See him? Here. Yesterday afternoon, here, about half past five."

"Exactly here?"

"Along there in the works. Excuse me, I must go and see him."

"I'll take you there," said Martineau. "Get your coat."

Ben turned and re-entered the garage. The three policemen followed him. They looked around. There were four funeral cars and a hearse, a pickup truck, a bigger truck, a brake, or station wagon, with opaque windows, a small van, and a Ford Consul saloon. All ten vehicles were in shining condition.

"My men will have to look round this place," Martineau said. "Do you mind?"

"No. Take me to Dad."

"Will you leave your keys with them? You can collect them when I bring you back."

Ben took a large bunch of keys from his pocket and gave them to Devery. "Let's go," he said.

In the car he stared sightlessly at the windscreen. Martineau said, "You mustn't mind my questions. Was your father all right when he left you yesterday afternoon?"

"Yes. Yes. He was as right as rain."

"What were you talking about?"

"I don't know. Business. We're partners. It was just chatter."

"Try to remember."

"Well, oh, we talked about the invoice for some West African mahogany. We've been using that lately for coffins. He said the price was ruinous, but he says that about everything. He can never take it in that things are going up."

"Anything else?"

"He asked me what I'd be doing later, and I said I didn't know. I had no arrangements."

"Anything else?"

"No. I don't think—a call came in for a laying-out job. I took it, and Dad went home." There was a break in Ben's voice as he added, "And that's the last I saw of him."

"You went on this laying-out job?"

"Yes."

"What is the procedure?"

"Well, we go—I get the coffin board and put it in the brake, and go and pick up Mrs. Hall, who lays out for us. Then, well, we go and do the job."

"How long did it take you?"

"Oh, a couple of hours, maybe. Last night it was just turned eight o'clock when I got home. Mrs. Harrison, that's the house-keeper, told me he'd gone to the Gee Gee Club."

"Your father was a widower?"

"Um. Yes. For the last ten years."

"And did he usually tell the housekeeper where he was going?"

"I don't know. But he always tells her on Saturdays. He takes over Saturdays at six, if anything comes in. He does Sundays too, as a rule. That's to give me a break. I'm on call every other night in the week."

"I see. I must ask you this. What did you do after eight o'clock last night?"

"I had a bath and a meal. That made it about nine. I watched the telly for half an hour. Then I went to the Dusty Miller and sat with the lads in the taproom for an hour or so.

73

I think I stayed till eleven o'clock. Then I came home, read the evening paper, went to bed."

"Yes. I'll have to verify all this, you know. Routine."

"I suppose you have. That's all right with me."

Martineau had driven slowly, in order to talk. Now when they arrived at the mortuary, Ben seemed inclined to hang back. Martineau understood. He had seen that curious reluctance in other people, in similar circumstances.

He was holding Ben gently by the arm when he took him to the corpse. He uncovered the face. "Do you formally identify this body?" he asked.

Ben nodded. He seemed to be choking.

"As Webster Olney?"

The bereaved son realized that he had to speak up. "Yes," he managed to say.

Martineau pulled the body's covering down to the waist. He said, "That's what he died of."

Ben stared down at the wounds. They were not stiletto wounds; the knife had had a broad blade. Gradually, a change came over him. "The bastards," he whispered. "The dirty bastards."

Martineau was watching him closely. "Have you some idea who did this?" he wanted to know.

Ben turned and stared blindly at him. "Bastards," he said. Then he swung right around and rushed unsteadily out of the building.

ELEVEN

Ben was striding away from the hospital, apparently with no destination in mind, when Martineau overtook him in the car. He stopped and called to him. His voice was peremptory. Ben came and got into the car. In silence the two men rode back to the Olney Works.

As the car stopped, Devery came out of the garage. "Ah, I'm glad you've brought Mr. Olney back," he said. "I want him to look at something."

He led the way to the brake. The double-leaf door at the back was standing open. A side door also was open, and Ainslie was searching around the front seats. He was wearing a pair of old motoring gloves which he had found.

In the back of the brake the extra seats lay flat. Devery pointed. On one of the seats, and on the floor beside it, there were a number of brown stains. Some of them were little dried-up pools, others were no more than smears. Martineau peered at them, and nodded.

"Do you know anything about those stains?" he asked Ben.

"No," the young man said. "No. They weren't there yesterday. At least I didn't notice them."

"Do you use this for moving bodies?"

"Yes. Is that blood? You know we don't move bleeding bodies."

"You used this vehicle yesterday evening?"

"I did. I brought it in just before eight, when I'd finished that laying-out job."

"Did you check the mileage?"

"No. Why? Only my father and I use it as a rule. We don't bother to keep a record of mileage."

"Right," said Martineau. "You're not looking too good. Go outside and get some air. Try a cigarette. But don't go away."

Ben nodded thankfully and went out. Martineau said to Ainslie, "Stand at the door and keep an eye on him. I think he's in a state of shock."

Ainslie also went away. "Shock?" Devery said. "I thought he was taking it very well."

"I want him out of the way for a minute, but within reach. Now, what about this blood, if it is blood? Dead bodies don't bleed so much."

"Death might not have been instantaneous."

"Perhaps not. It looks as if Olney was taken to the mortuary in the brake. He might have been stripped here, or on the way there. If they didn't leave his clothes somewhere there, they'd bring them back here. They might be on the premises."

"Are they important?"

"Yes. If his money and his watch were taken, it's capital murder. It's about time Rapp shook hands with the hangman. He'll never be anything but a menace."

There was a telephone on a rough unpainted table near the door. Martineau called the hospital, and spoke to Sergeant Bird. "When you've finished there, come over here," he said. "The Olney Cabinet Works, Rowan Street, Mossbank."

When the call had been made, Martineau called Ben in and toured the entire premises with him. The workshop was impressive, filled with modern woodworking machinery and finished or unfinished doors, window frames, coffins, tables and other articles of furniture.

"How many men do you employ?" Martineau asked.

"Men and boys, eighteen. And one woman in the office," Ben replied.

The office was a glass-partitioned room in a corner of the big shed. Martineau looked in, glanced round, and made a mental note to have the books examined.

From the workshop they went to the funeral parlor, going round it to enter by the front door. The doctor's old house had been kept in good condition, and flowers bloomed in a basket which hung in the stone porch. The largest ground-floor room had been equipped with chairs and a lectern, so that burial services could be held there. The remaining rooms each had a bier, so that bodies could lie in state while awaiting burial or cremation. There were flowers in every room, and the air was heavy with their scent. Martineau commented on this.

"It costs us pounds a week for flowers, besides what folk send," Ben told him.

Martineau was looking at a door at the back of the hall. "Cellar?" he asked.

"That's right. There's a lot of useless old stuff the doctor's lot left behind. We've never bothered to move it."

They went into the cellar and saw unwanted furniture which had been in small rear bedrooms in the days when there were servants in the house. There was quite a lot of it, and also a few items which had once been treasured possessions of the lady of the house. There was a lacquered screen and a marble clock and a cane table. All were covered with dust. Martineau did not envy the men who would have to search there.

They returned to the main floor. There were two bodies in coffins on the biers. Martineau looked at them, asked about them, and about the accommodation of bodies generally.

"Three is about average," Ben told him. "We've room for five down here and three upstairs. It's very seldom we have to put any upstairs."

"What else is upstairs?"

"Not a thing."

"I'll have a look at it," said Martineau dryly.

Ben led the way upstairs. As he had stated, three of the rooms contained biers, and the rest, except for an accumulation of dust, were quite empty. They were still adorned with the doctor's wallpaper. Everywhere the dust was undisturbed.

Martineau appeared to be satisfied with what he had seen,

but he had not quite finished with Ben. "Have you told me everything you know?" he asked.

"Yes."

"Have you reason to suspect any particular person or persons of killing your father?"

"No. I wish I had."

"Did he have any enemies?"

"No. None that I know of."

"At the mortuary you referred to certain bastards. In the plural. Why?"

Ben looked at the policeman in surprise. "Because they are bastards," he said. "As for the plural, it never occurred to me that one man could have done the whole thing by himself."

Martineau nodded. "Can you think of any reason *why* anyone would want to murder your father?"

"No, I can't. Unless it was to rob him."

"Did he carry much money?"

"He might have had ten pounds, or even twenty. He wouldn't have more than that."

"What else in the way of personal property?"

"He had a Longines wrist watch, solid gold. On a leather strap. It was worth about a hundred pounds."

"What else?"

"Oh, a bunch of keys like mine. A Ronson lighter. Cigarettes, happen. Diary and that. Specs in a case."

"Optician's name inside the case?"

"I don't know. I never noticed. He usually went to Sawyer, in Petersgate."

"Right, we'll go down," said Martineau. He left Ben in the garage with Devery, and took Ainslie with him to Webster Olney's house in Highfield. He found that it was a detached house of modest size, in a condition which indicated that the owner had never been short of the price of a coat of paint. The door was opened by a stout, red-faced woman.

Martineau learned that she was Mrs. Harrison, the housekeeper. He also learned that she had been employed at the house for less than a year, so that in her case deep personal feelings would not be involved. Nevertheless, he was as tactful as possible in telling her that she had recently been deprived of an employer.

She was more surprised than distressed. Like Ben, she had

been under the impression that Webster Olney was in his bed. "I were just thinkin' it were time he got up," she said.

Martineau questioned her. As far as it went, her story corroborated Ben's. In any case, the detective had no suspicion of Ben. He was merely following his normal routine of exploring every avenue, leaving no stone unturned, not trusting the Archbishop of Canterbury's daughter.

Mrs. Harrison's account of the phone call and its sequel was straightforward. "It were about twenty past ten when telephone rung," she said. "I took it, an' it were a man what said undertaker were wanted at 15 Warbeck Road. I ast where that were an' he said it were Dodsbury way. I ast who were dead an' he said Russell Perkins. I didn't ask who were callin'. Didn't think it mattered. Then I rang up the Gee Gee Club an' ast for Mr. Olney. When he come to the phone I gev him the message, an' he said, 'All right, I'll go.' He didn't seem too pleased."

"What would he do then?"

"Well, I only called him out once before from the club. He told me after as he'd gone to a taxi rank an' took a cab to the garridge, to get the brake out.

"How was Mr. Olney yesterday?"

"He were all right when he got up. He sat about reading the paper an' that, then he went potterin' off to the works. He seemed a bit gloomy an' tired like when he come back. I don't know what for. He doesn't do much work. Ben does nearly all the work, an' he works long hours, very hard."

"Thank you, Mrs. Harrison. Now I'm going to ask you to let me take a quick look round. Then I'll leave this officer here to see that nothing in the house outside the kitchen is taken away or disturbed. A search crew will arrive later. I'm sorry to be a nuisance, but all this is necessary routine."

Inquiries were made at 15 Warbeck Road, Dodsbury. Nobody called Russell Perkins was known there, and no Russell Perkins had lived there for ten years at least. All the Perkinses in the Post Office directory and the Burgess Roll could not produce a Russell. It became a reasonable certainty that Russell Perkins had been the product of somebody's imagination.

Inquiries were made at the taxi rank some two hundred and

fifty yards away from the Gee Gee Club. A driver remembered taking Mr. Olney from the rank to the Olney Works soon after half past ten on Saturday night. He knew Mr. Olney, who often took a cab from the rank when he was leaving the club. The last he had seen of Mr. Olney was after he had alighted from the cab. He had been walking through the works gateway toward the garage, sorting out a key from a biggish bunch of keys.

Inquiries were made all along the half mile of quiet streets between the Olney Works and the Olney home. The undertaker had been in a good mood when he left his son at the works, and he had been worried or depressed on his arrival home and for several hours later. This conclusion was based on the statements of people who might have been mistaken. And it was also possible that the man might have been upset by nothing more serious than a headache. All the same, the inquiries were pursued. On that short journey, made on foot, something could have happened to upset him. Whatever it was, the police wanted to know.

The mortuary, the whole of the Olney Works, and the Olney home were thoroughly searched. The search produced nothing of importance except the bloodstains in the brake and a great number of fingerprints. These had to be sorted and classified. Later, one or two of them might be important.

A search was made for Webster Olney's clothes, and for the contents of his pockets. Somebody—Cassidy it was—remarked that anybody going from the Olney Works to the General Hospital would have to pass over the Fosse Canal at some place. Martineau looked at the map. Either of two bridges could have been used. He made arrangements for the canal to be dragged near both bridges. After only a few minutes' work under the interested gaze of Sunday afternoon strollers, a sodden bundle of clothes was brought to the surface. Martineau was called to the scene. He cut the knotted length of shoe laces and tie which held the bundle together, and found a complete outfit: shirt, underclothes, socks, trousers, coat, waistcoat, shoes, and a squashed, shapeless hat. The shoes were in the heart of the bundle, and wedged into each one there was a broken brick.

Martineau looked at the halves of brick. "I think these will be Verney Barton's clothes," he said. "If they dumped Verney's clothes here, and they hadn't been found, they might have thought it a good spot to dump Olney's. Keep on dragging."

In the pockets of the suit there was everything a man would normally carry, except money. Martineau nodded grimly. It had been murder in the furtherance of theft; a hanging matter for which there would never be a conviction. He left the clothes lying on the towpath and watched the salvage operations.

Half an hour later a second bundle of clothes was brought up. Like the first one, it was a complete outfit and was tied in the same manner. To sink the bundle, spanners had been put inside the shoes, and beside them were two tire levers and a big wrench. "I expect these will be Olney's," Martineau said. "These tools would be taken from the brake."

Olney's pockets had not been emptied, but his money had been taken. Also, apparently, his watch had been taken. Even with £29,000 at stake, Ernie Rapp would not miss the chance of acquiring a fine gold watch. Martineau was pleased about that. The watch might hang Ernie.

Now the uniformed sergeant in charge of the salvage was like a hound on the scent. He lugged a big submersible magnet to the edge of the water and forcefully instructed his men in the use of it. Martineau was excited, too. He lit a cigarette and smoked it down to a stub in about two minutes.

The magnet brought up a number of things: rusty nails, pieces of rotten wood with nails embedded, one hobnailed boot and then another, one very rusty ice skate, and finally a prize. It was the sheath of a knife, and its steel rim and tip were not rusty at all. It could have been in the water only a few hours.

The sheath was carefully dropped from the magnet on to Martineau's spread handkerchief. He tied the corners of the handkerchief and handed it to Cassidy. He lit another cigarette, and before he had smoked it the magnet brought up the knife. That also had been in the water only a few hours.

When the knife was hanging in Cassidy's handkerchief, Martineau urged the uniformed sergeant to continue his operations until he was satisfied that there was no more metal within a stone's throw of the canal bridge. Then he departed with his exhibits. It had been a profitable afternoon.

TWELVE

THE OTHER SIDE

"I'M SORRY, kid, really am," Lew Cory murmured, on the telephone. "It was an accident. He started to kick up a dust before we could talk to him. Somebody was a bit too quick quietenin' him. I'm not sayin' who it was."

Ben's only comment was a dissatisfied grunt. This was not a private line, and one could not be too careful. Besides, he was still undecided about the attitude he would take up toward the men who had murdered his father.

"It's bad, I know," Cory soothed. "But it might not be altogether a bad thing. You'd had it with him. He might have altered his will and left everything to a dogs' home. You know. As it is, you'll be all right."

Ben grunted again, this time slightly mollified. His sense of bereavement was already assuaged by a certain relief. The problem of his father was solved, and the police would never suspect him, the only son, of having had anything to do with the solving. He had not looked forward to the long patient effort which would have been necessary to regain his father's forgiveness and trust. God knows what his father might have thought up. Also, the Northern Steel money was still safe, and now it would not need to be moved.

Nevertheless, Ben did not think it was right for him to let Cory become aware of his relief. He had to make some sort of protest. He had his pride. He was not going to let them deliberately kill his father and think that he would be satisfied with a few words of apology.

"Did you intend it, from the start?" he asked bitterly. "I'll bet you did."

"Christ Almighty, kid! Us knowin' what he was to you?"

That was Cory, still solemnly going through the motions. Cory, showing a little decent feeling. Cory!

"It's the way you did it," Ben growled. "Using my own trick on my own flesh and blood. *That* was clever of you, I *must* say. Using the same gag twice."

Cory remained contrite, apparently determined not to rebut any of Ben's comments at this time. "It wasn't good," he admitted. "But it did seem a good idea at the time. We were rushed, you know. It wasn't as if we'd planned it that way."

"It wasn't a brilliant idea to use the vehicle you did, either. What's the matter—couldn't you have got a car somewhere?"

"I tell you, kid, we hadn't the time. My oppo on the job was bein' looked for."

"All right. All right. Tomorrow as arranged," Ben said, and rang off. He had to make his protest without committing himself. He had uttered no word which might suggest either acceptance or forgiveness. Let them worry a bit.

Now Ben was sure that he knew the answer to his question; murder had been in Cory's mind a minute after he had learned that the Northern Steel plunder was in jeopardy. He had decided that an old man with a conscience about property could never be trusted to remain silent, even after being made to see reason. Furthermore, Cory had been quick to see the possibility of disinheritance. He had not wanted Ben to be cut out of his father's will. He had wanted Ben to be expectant of a legacy and secure in the ownership of a valuable business, so anchored by self-interest that even a sum like £29,000 would not tempt him to run away. So he had made sure that Ben would inherit.

"Thanks, Cory," Ben murmured savagely. "I won't forget. If ever I get the chance, I'll push you into trouble right up to the eyes."

Cory was savage too, as he walked away from the telephone box. Conciliation was very contrary to his nature.

"Thinks he's clever," he fumed. "He had to come to me to help him out, and I did him a good turn. Set him up for life, I did. And all he does is moan. All right, we'll see who's the clever one."

He began to consider the possibility of blackmailing Ben when all was over, when the Northern Steel money had been spent.

THIRTEEN

AT HEADQUARTERS, Martineau found Sergeant Bird in the room which he called his laboratory. He was still working on the fingerprints he had found. He looked up with a scowl when the two detectives entered. The scowl remained even when he saw that one of the detectives was a chief inspector. He was tired and he was busy, and he liked people to knock before they entered.

The sodden clothes had been left in Martineau's office. He and Cassidy were carrying respectively a knife and sheath, each in a slung handkerchief.

"Sergeant," he said. "I've heard that fingerprints can remain on an object even after submersion in water."

Bird sniffed. "That's common knowledge, sir."

Martineau found a clear place on the table and opened the handkerchief. "See what you can do with that, then."

"H'm. A Boy Scout's knife."

"A Bowie knife it is," said Cassidy. "The lad who used that has never been a Boy Scout."

"Is this the murder weapon?"

"We think so," said Martineau. "We'd like to be able to prove it."

85

Bird picked up the knife with his forceps. He pulled down an adjustable light. He peered. "There's still some blood on this, where the blade joins the hilt," he said.

He carried the knife to a small table in the corner and did some careful puffing with an insufflator. He returned, and dropped the knife point down onto the handkerchief. "Clean, except for the blood," he said.

Martineau was not disappointed, because good fingerprints on a murder weapon were something to dream about and seldom a reality. "All right," he said. "Have a look at the sheath."

Bird looked at the sheath, and sniffed again. "Leather," he growled. Then he looked again, and more closely. "I don't believe it is leather," he said. "It looks like a superior sort of plastic."

He carried the sheath to the corner table, and he was smiling when he returned with it. He held it under the light. Limned in light gray powder on the black plastic was a clear thumbprint. With a flick of his forceps he turned it over, and four blurred fingerprints could be seen.

"The thumbprint's a good 'un," said Bird, happy now. "And I think I've got another one just like it. It's one I found in the brake. It was in the usual place. When he wiped the car down he forgot he'd adjusted the driving mirror to suit his height."

Martineau was happy too. "The same print on the sheath and in the brake ties it up nicely," he said. "When will you be able to show me?"

"Half an hour."

"Right." Martineau picked up the knife. "You won't want this."

He returned to his office, thoughtfully weighing the knife in his hand. Because it was Sunday, he could not send detectives around the hardware shops to discover who stocked that particular brand of Sheffield steel. But there was something he could do.

"I wouldn't be surprised if this knife was pinched from some place," he said to Cassidy. "Make a note of this trademark, then go up to Records and on my instructions have them start looking for such a knife on their lists of property not recovered. Stay and help, just to make sure they get on with the job."

Cassidy went on his errand. Martineau entered his office. He telephoned a description of the knife to the front office, with a request that it should be circulated throughout the force, and an instruction that any officer remembering such a knife being listed in stolen property must report to the C.I.D. at once. Then, to be thorough, he communicated with the Lost Property Department to find out if the knife, or one like it, had been reported as lost.

While he waited, the chief inspector sent for Mrs. Barton and for Ben Olney. Ben arrived first. He nodded sadly when Martineau showed him his father's clothes. He looked at the tools, and nodded again. "We did have a wrench like that in the brake, and the others look familiar," he said. "I'll have a checkup and see what's missing."

Martineau let him go as Mrs. Barton arrived. She identified Verney's clothes immediately and positively, and went away weeping. Martineau was depressed as he reflected that he had moved a step further in the matter of establishing Verney's death. He sent both sets of clothes to the police forensic laboratory.

He took the tools along to Bird's office and saw two blown-up pictures of two thumbprints. They looked exactly alike to him, and Bird assured him that they were, both in classification and in individual characteristics.

"But they aren't on our records," he said. "I'll get the inquiries off to Scotland Yard and Wakefield tonight. One of them might have a record."

Martineau nodded. He told Bird where the tools had been found, and then he went away. The thumbprints were not Ernie Rapp's, at any rate, because Ernie's fingerprints, palm prints, and all other prints were in the local files. He wondered if he ought to have Rapp picked up for interrogation, and then send men with a warrant to search his house. One main objection to such a move was that interrogation of Rapp was a waste of time. Well, it would be unnecessary if the little thief happened to have Olney's watch in his possession. Martineau doubted that he would be such a fool. The watch would be hidden somewhere.

Shortly after seven o'clock a rush of news enabled him to make up his mind. When the public houses opened for the curtailed Sunday evening period, Long Cue Lancaster had eluded his shadow by means of the front-door back-door trick. Half an hour later, Ernie Rapp had slipped his leash by the same method. It was also reported that George ("Waddy") Waddington and Redvers ("Ruby") Atkins had been seen several times in the last hour, and it was thought that they might have been stalking Rapp.

Martineau gave his orders to Devery. "I want Rapp and Lancaster," he said. "And I want a search of Rapp's place and Lancaster's lodgings. The chief's warrant will do for those two characters. See to it."

Devery hurried away. Martineau sat and rubbed his chin, and thought about Ruby Atkins and Waddy. Their appearance on the scene was unwelcome, most unwelcome. They foreshadowed trouble of a sort which he feared. He had been aware of other men in the city who would be pondering as seriously as himself about the hiding place of the Northern Steel plunder. Dixie Costello would have his ear to the ground. Both ears if he could manage it. There were also boss mobsters of lesser caliber than Dixie, and in addition a number of talented lone wolves. With subterranean diligence they would be seeking an opportunity to rob the robbers. Each of them would have the figure of £29,000 burning in his mind like a neon sign.

There was a likelihood that one of these criminals would locate the £29,000 before the police could do so. They had sources of information, and means of extorting it, which were denied to the police. Take Dixie Costello. Dixie's boys were on chatting terms with all kinds of crooks, with informers, with the betting fraternity and its dishonest fringe, with the innkeepers and club owners who leaned casually on their bars and heard many secrets. A question from one of Dixie's men would be answered freely. The same question uttered by a detective officer would be answered by a blank stare or a shake of the head. If Dixie thought that any man knew where the Northern Steel money was hidden, he would take him and twist his arm twice round his head, backwards. The police could not do that.

Ruby Atkins and Waddy were two of Dixie's men. Their presence in Rapp's vicinity might be a matter of chance or it might mean that Dixie had scented his prey. Martineau thought he knew, now, why Rapp had eluded his observers a second time. He had not been disturbed by policemen on his tail, because he had assumed that he would be able to slip away from them at any time. But he had certainly been disturbed by the sight of Ruby and Waddy. That was why he had vanished from sight and, probably, gone to earth somewhere. And it was quite likely that before he did so he had been able to warn Long Cue Lancaster of the new danger.

Martineau knew perfectly well that if Dixie Costello once put his hands on the Northern Steel money, it might well be lost. Costello's affairs and concerns, legitimate and otherwise, had so many ramifications that he was able to channel away hot money with a degree of safety. Only once had he ever been interrupted on such an operation, and even then the police had been unable to build up a case against him.

The chief inspector's chain of thought was broken by the whir of the telephone. The call was from a detective sergeant attached to a division which was mainly residential. He remembered a Sunday afternoon break-in at the home of one Cyril Merrick, a young married man who had been a Rover Scout. The house, temporarily unoccupied, had been ransacked. Among the property stolen had been a Bowie knife of the same make and description as the knife which had been fished out of the Fosse Canal. At the time of the theft, Merrick had mentioned the loss of the knife not because of its value but because he was afraid that in the hands of a bad character it might be misused. "I don't want any stabbings laid at my door," he had remarked.

"Was the job cleared?" Martineau asked the detective sergeant.

"Yes, sir. Taken into consideration with a few more jobs. But the knife was not among the property recovered."

"On whose record was it?"

"Andy Persons."

"Ah," said Martineau with satisfaction. Andrew Persons was a character so slippery that he was known to the police, inevitably, as Missing Persons. But he was neither brave nor reticent. When in danger, he would sing for his succor.

"When was this?" the chief inspector asked.

"A year last Christmas. Persons got twelve months."

"So he's out and about. I'm assuming that you cleared the

the job. Did you ask Persons about the knife?"

"I'm afraid I didn't, sir. There was stuff of much greater value involved. All I know is that he didn't have the knife when we did his drum. He must have either sold it or lost it."

"He'll tell us what he did with it. Does this Merrick still live on your manor?"

"Yes, sir. I see him quite often."

"Take a car and see how soon you can get him down here," said Martineau, concluding the talk. Then, to save time, he put out the word for Persons.

When Merrick arrived, Martineau showed him the Bowie knife. He handled it, turned it over, and said quite positively, "Yes, that's my knife."

"How can you tell?"

"I started to cut notches in the handle for every foreign country I visited when I was a Scout. But I found this black stuff on the handle was too hard. I couldn't even cut it with a razor blade, so I gave it up. There's just one little notch and a few scratches where the razor blade slipped. The scratches are still there, see. I'd know the knife anywhere."

"Good enough. You might be required to testify."

"But I thought the man had already been sent to prison."

"He was, but the knife was not among the property recovered. Now it's been used to kill somebody."

"Oh, Lor'! My knife. You're certain?"

"Reasonably certain."

"Oh dear. That's what I was afraid might happen."

"No need for you to worry. The killing was premeditated. If it hadn't been your knife, it would have been some other. They wouldn't have been stopped by the lack of any particular knife."

Merrick was relieved to hear that and went away somewhat comforted. Martineau picked up the telephone and gave orders which would put more men on the search for Missing Persons. Then, thinking that he had earned it, he slipped out for a pint of ale.

When he returned to the C.I.D. he found Persons waiting for him, under the care of the uniformed constable who had picked him up in the street near his home. He was chewing his nails unhappily, no doubt wondering which one of his misdeeds was about to be brought home to him.

Martineau looked at him, looked him up and down, and nodded grimly. "So you've eventually come to it," he said heavily. "Your last tickle."

Persons looked alarmed, but before he could speak, Martineau went on, "Come into my office and I'll show you something."

When he was seated at his desk, with Persons standing before him, he took the murder knife from a drawer and slid it along the desk. Persons gazed at it in silence.

"It's just been identified," the policeman said. "It was stolen by you from the house of Mr. Cyril Merrick, 28 Lea Drive, Dartlea, a year last Christmas."

"Well, I admitted the job. It was took into consideration. I done my time."

"Yes, but this knife was never recovered from you."

"What of it? It's recovered now."

"Yes, from the Fosse Canal. After it had been used to murder a man. If it hadn't been Sunday, you'd have been able to read about it in the evening paper."

Persons looked stricken. "I never had naught to do wi' no murder," he shouted in a panic.

"The evidence of the knife indicates that you did."

"I didn't. I lost that knife the day after I got it. Somebody pinched it off me."

"Who?"

"I don't know."

"Not good enough. I've got the knife and I've got you. You're the goat."

"You can't prove I did a murder!"

"Can't I? Don't kid yourself. I'll find all the evidence I need."

"Look, just when was this murder?"

"You should know. You did it."

"No, I didn't, no, I didn't! I tell you I had that knife less'n twenty-four hours. Somebody huffed it."

"If you're trying to tell me somebody burgled that crummy dump you call home, you're further in the muck than ever."

"I'm not. It were took off me."

"Larceny from the Persons. You'll have to give some convincing detail to put that one over."

"It were in the public bar at the Engineers' Arms, Boxing Day. The very day after I done the Dartlea job. I were fooling about wi' the knife, sticking it in the bar top, an' that. A fellow there said, 'That's a nice knife,' an' he just picked it up. He took the sheath out of me hand, an' all. Said he might as well have it."

"What time of day was this?"

"Just before I went to me dinner. A quarter to one, happen."

"Who was this fellow?"

"I don't know."

"Didn't you do anything about it?"

"No. How could I? He had it. I daren't start a barney about it, because I'd pinched it meself. I just had to let it go."

"He sounds like a cool hand."

"He is."

"Ah. You know him."

Persons knew that he had slipped. "I don't know him. I've seen him the odd time since."

Martineau shook his head. "You can do better than that. You're good enough for me to hold. I'm going to hold you till you tell me this fellow's name or until you admit he doesn't exist. Constable, take him down, and lock him up."

But Persons did not want to be taken down. He resisted. "Wait a minute!" he cried. "It was Lew Cory took that knife off me."

Martineau nodded to the P. C., and Persons was released.

"Why didn't you tell me the first time?" the chief inspector demanded. "Are you afraid of Cory?"

"Not exactly flayed. . . . Yes, dammit, I am. I'm scared to death of him."

"As bad as that, is he?"

"I'm not sayin'. Only he flays me."

"Well, we'll spread it out a bit. There must have been witnesses. You couldn't have been alone with him in a public bar on Boxing Day."

"Well, I remember Ted Moore bein' there. An' Nellie the

landlady. She'll happen remember who else was there."

"She'll get the chance. Now tell me about this Lew Cory."

"He's a hard case. A big, strong bloke. Hard-faced, he is. Nasty. He looks like a man who'd save it up for you."

"He won't save it this time. He'll be too busy. I want a statement from you. All you can remember about Cory and the knife. You'll give it to this officer before you leave here. Then you'll keep quiet about it."

"You bet I will," Persons replied fervently. "But what about Nellie? She'll talk. And so will Moore, happen. Cory 'ull get to know."

Martineau thought about that. "All right, I'll take a chance that you're telling the truth. I won't approach Moore and the landlady until I've got Cory right. So the whole thing can be kept squat. Has he got a police record?"

"I don't know. I haven't been much in his company. He's not the sort of man I like to have around me."

"Where does he live?"

"I don't know, an' that's honest truth."

"What does he do for a living, when he's working?"

"I don't know that either. I got the impression he had summat to do wi' the bookies."

"Mmmm. Does he go to the dogs?"

"Yes, he does."

"The City Greyhound Stadium or the Summerfield Arena?"

"Both, I expect. I've seen him at the Stadium. Come to think of it, I see him nearly every time I go there."

"Who are his friends?"

"I don't think he has any."

"Have you never seen him with anybody?"

"Not actually *with* anybody. He seems to go about on his own."

"You can do better than that. Every man has a friend somewhere."

"You don't know Cory. He's not like an ordinary fellow."

"What about women? Who's his woman?"

Persons shook his head. "He's a flashy dresser. That sort generally likes a woman. But I've never seen him with one."

"All right. What does he look like?"

Persons gave a description of Cory. It was a vivid verbal picture of a cold-eyed brute.

"What does he usually wear?" Martineau pursued.

"Oh, he's a proper Dale Street dandy. Light trilby, light suit, nice crease in his trousers. He always looks as if he's going to the races on his day off."

"You mentioned Dale Street. What put that into your mind?"

"Oh, he talks with a bit of a Liverpool twang."

"All right. Give your statement to the constable, then you can go."

Thankfully Persons departed with the P. C. When they had gone, Martineau put an inquiry through to his own C.R.O., and to the Liverpool City Police, to learn if anything was known of Lewis Cory. But he did not put out a general inquiry to the Granchester force. He did not want Cory to be forewarned because some officer had mentioned the man's name to the wrong person. For that reason he did not telephone any of the bookmakers he knew.

As an afterthought, he looked at the membership list of the Gee Gee Club. Cory's name was on the list. The only address given was Granchester.

"So he'll be known at the club," the chief inspector mused. "Well, I can't ask Gee or Wragg to finger him for me."

There was the girl, Cleo Patton, taking up one man's time. Ainslie still thought that she was genuine. Ainslie could be right or he could be wrong. She might help or she might give Cory the tip-off. Chances like that had to be taken. Martineau thought briefly about exposing the girl to reprisals, and reassured himself. The thing would be done discreetly. In any case, she could have police protection.

In view of the evident danger, he decided that it would not be fair to ask Ainslie to recruit Miss Patton's services. He found her number in the telephone book, and dialed it. The girl herself answered the call.

Martineau gave his name. "Have you heard about Webster Olney?" he asked.

"Yes," she replied. "Joe—P. C. Ainslie—told me."

"Olney was a friend of yours?"

"Yes."

"With regard to his murder, would you be willing to help the police?"

"Yes."

"Do you know a man called Lewis Cory?"

"I know him by sight."

"Well enough to point him out to a policeman?"

"Yes."

"Would you do it?"

"Yes."

"There just might be a chance of danger for you, but we will do our best to keep you out of sight. We will also protect you if necessary. I want you to understand that."

"I understand."

"Is he a man you would be afraid of?"

"Yes. I've never had any dealings with him, but I'm afraid of him."

"But you'll go through with it?"

"Yes."

Well, thought Martineau as he put down the receiver, you ask a straight question and get a straight answer. It was beginning to look as if young Ainslie's judgment of feminine character was pretty good.

FOURTEEN

AT TWENTY minutes past seven on Monday night, Joe Ainslie paid expense money at a City Stadium turnstile, for Cleo and himself to enter. Inside, he bought two race cards. It was already quite dark, a black night which promised rain, and under a glare of lights the bookmakers were bawling the odds for the first race. Already many people were standing on the wide, sloping concourse in front of the bookies and the tote, but Joe and Cleo took up their position in a comparatively unlighted spot behind them, at the end of the line.

It was the first time Joe had ever been to a greyhound racing track. He gazed around, at the grandstand, at the brilliantly lit circuit, at the shouting bookmakers, at the tote, at the refreshment bar, at the box in which the judge was safely out of reach of the crowd should he make an unpopular decision, and finally, with approval, at his companion.

Cleo was dressed for the occasion in a belted raincoat which fitted her perfectly, flat-heeled shoes, and a headscarf. It was a big scarf, and she had arranged it so that the lower part of her face was covered. She might have been a young woman of social standing who did not wish to be recognized at the dog track or she might have been a married woman who also had reasons for not being recognized. Naturally, roving eyes noticed the perfect figure in the raincoat, and of course they also noticed the face covering. But at a dog track the pursuit of Lady Luck is an exclusive appetite. Cleo was seen, briefly wondered about, and forgotten.

She was nervous, but determined. Soon after her meeting with Joe she had made up her mind that she would not be a police informer even to help him in his career. But the murder of Webster Olney had changed all that. Such a nice, harmless old man! It seemed to her almost as bad as the murder of a child. There and then she had given Joe the only piece of information he had wanted from her. She had stated definitely that Olney had had money in his pocket when he left the club, because she had seen him change a five-pound note to pay for his last drink there. And she had known quite well what her evidence would help to prove, that Olney's murder was capital murder, a matter for the hangman.

Nervously, then, she looked around. She saw Martineau standing a few yards away. "There's your inspector," she said to Joe.

"Yes," Joe replied. "And that big fellow a bit farther back is Cassidy. And I saw Devery and Hearn in front there, moving into the crowd. I don't know how many more there are."

"I don't see anything of Cory yet. Wouldn't he be foolish to come here, if he's been a regular visitor?"

"Not really. It's likely he still thinks the police don't know he exists. So he'll assume there's no need to lie doggo or change his habits. He'll just go wherever he wants to go."

"Should we move around?"

"No. Martineau said not. If he's here, he'll come to place a bet eventually. We'll just move along till we're between the bookies and the tote."

They moved, and waited. The crowd became thicker and the bookies noisier and busier. The tote windows also became busy places. Joe consulted his card, and moved a short distance to a window and placed a five-shilling bet on No. 2, Oakland Boy.

Cleo did not see the man she was looking for. Joe said, "He might be among the crowd, or he might arrive here later. Some of the wide boys come here to back one dog in one race, and one only. We— Hello!"

The first race had started. The electric hare fled round the track, and five greyhounds raced after it. Number 3, Percy Vere, was the winner. "I never do have any luck gambling," Joe said.

People who had backed the winning hound swarmed briefly around tote and bookies, then there was comparative peace. But soon bookies began to chalk up the runners of the next race, shouting the odds as they did so. A few early backers strolled up, looking for the best odds on certain dogs. These were the people who had made up their minds hours ago. Possibly they had information, and were preparing to back their selections before there was any chance of heavy money shortening the odds.

"I think I'll stick to Number Two," Joe was saying, when Cleo put a hand on his arm.

"He's there, I think," she said quietly.

A big man, looking bigger in a very clean, very light raincoat, had come from the direction of the stand. Entering the area of bright lights, he approached the first bookmaker and stopped to look at his board. He was at the other end of the long line and, furthermore, the brim of his raffish but immaculate hat shadowed the upper part of his face.

"I'd better make sure," Cleo breathed.

She walked away swiftly, passing behind the long row of Old Firms and Honest Johns. Joe strode along at her elbow, muttering a plea for her to be careful, take it easy, don't muff it.

When they reached the other end of the line, the big man had made his bet and was turning away from the bookmaker. It must have been a heavy bet, because the bookie was changing the odds on No. 2, The Dart. When the big man was in plain view Joe caught Cleo's arm and pulled her back. The man glanced in their direction, and saw them both looking at him. They had muffed it.

They both realized it, but they made a pretense of having no interest in the man. Cleo looked down at her race card and murmured: "That's Lew Cory."

Cory had stopped. He was watching them, and he was very alert indeed. From them his glance slid around, but at first he saw nothing to alarm him. He returned to his study of Joe and

Cleo. Joe looked up and gave him a brief, hostile glance, as a man will when he is being stared at by a stranger.

Apparently satisfied, Cory started to move away. But as he did so he looked around in another direction and noticed two tall figures moving through the crowd on a line parallel to the one he intended to take. The two were Devery and Hearn, keeping their distance and trying to get ahead of him. Cleo's sudden move and sudden stop had marked him for them as clearly as if she had pointed at him.

Seeing Devery and Hearn, but apparently still not quite sure that anything was amiss, Cory moved so that he could look behind the row of bookmakers' stands. He saw Cassidy standing with his back turned and hiding most of Martineau, who seemed to be in conversation with him. The general situation, and the shape and style of the last two, must have made all Cory's instincts shout "Copper!" He turned and ran toward the stand.

Joe started after him, and then stopped. His orders were definite—to stay with Cleo. Martineau and Cassidy went pounding by. Devery and Hearn closed in from the concourse.

Cory reached the front steps of the stand some ten yards ahead of Hearn, his nearest pursuer. The gatekeeper on duty there must have known him. He did nothing to obstruct him, but looked surprised and a little indignant at his haste. When Hearn arrived, the gatekeeper put out a hesitant, detaining hand which was brushed aside. When Devery arrived a second later he perceived the nature of the chase, and stepped out of the way.

Cory went bounding up to the highest, rearmost seats of the sparsely occupied stand, and then he raced along the gallery behind the last row of seats. Hearn and Devery followed. Martineau, at the gate below, stopped to look up and consider the general position. "Round the back," he said tersely to Cassidy. He pointed. The two men ran in different directions to the back of the stand.

Up on the top gallery of the stand, Cory reached an opening which led to some stairs going downward to a rear exit. He vanished into this, and his pursuers heard the slam of a door. When they reached the head of the stairs, he was not in sight.

They hurried down to the first landing, and found an unmarked door. Without a second's hesitation Hearn put the sole and heel of his shoe to it and burst it open. Devery rushed through the doorway. He found himself in a small washroom with another door. This was open, having a bolt only on the inner side, and it led to a narrow interior corridor with a closed door at the end. The place was dimly illuminated by one small, dusty bulb.

There were doors on either side of the corridor. "You go straight ahead," Devery said. "I'll try these places."

Hearn ran along to the closed door. It was barred against him, and moreover it was made to open toward him. A number of applications of his big foot were necessary to break a panel and reach the bar. When he got the door open he found that the corridor continued to the end of the structure, and at the end was a window. A wide flight of stairs crossed the corridor beside the shattered door.

The window was open. Hearn pondered briefly. The stairs were the obvious way out, but so had the other stairway been obvious. That window did not look right, somehow. He decided to look at the window first.

Martineau halted at the rear corner of the grandstand. From the corner he took a cautious look along the well-lit passage which separated the back of the stand from the perimeter wall of the Stadium. The passage was deserted. He waited, ready to move entirely out of sight should the fugitive appear. He could not see Cassidy at the other end, so he assumed that the Irishman also was peeping.

Martineau had waited thus for less than half a minute when he heard the grating noise of a rusty catch and hinges. He turned in surprise and glanced upward, and saw that a window in the end of the stand was opening outward. He slipped round the corner, out of sight of anyone who might obtrude his head to look down.

When he ventured to take a look, he saw a man climbing out the window. It was about twelve feet from the ground. The man suspended himself at arm's length from the sill, and dropped down onto the hard concrete. He landed lightly and came erect. He turned, and found himself facing Martineau.

"All right," the policeman said. "Steady does it." This was the man who had fled from him a minute or two ago. He had no doubt that it was Lew Cory.

He saw the white flash of Cory's grin. "You win," the man said. He came forward, and suddenly struck out. Martineau was not unprepared. He ducked, and counterpunched to the body. To his surprise the blow was blocked with professional ease, and then he was shaken by a hard right to the head. He clinched, realizing that he was going to take some punishment before help arrived. Well, a good hiding had to come some time. The man who had been the handiest battler in the Granchester police was past his prime. The reflexes of Chief Inspector Martineau were not the reflexes of young Constable Martineau.

The clinch was the signal for a knee to the groin, but Martineau was much too experienced to be caught by such a move. His own knee was in the way. From this phase of the action Cory was the first to get two feet on the ground again. He butted, aiming to smash Martineau's nose with his head. The policeman barely avoided that, and he had to come out of the clinch. There was an exchange of blows. If Martineau's right fist had reached its destination on time, the fracas would have been over. He hurt his opponent, but he did not really connect. On the other hand, Cory did connect with one masterly blow. Martineau's knees buckled. As he went down he went forward. Cory could have jumped away, and he should have done so. But for a split second he had forgotten that escape was his object, and he was coming in for the kill. Martineau's outstretched hands held him off. Those big hands slid down the front of Cory's coat, and grasped two handfuls of gabardine just above the knees. Himself on his knees, Martineau held on. Cory could not kick effectively, nor could he rid himself of his coat. He could only curse, and strike at the top of Martineau's head.

At the beginning of the chase, Joe and Cleo had walked toward the stand, both of them too excited and curious to remember that it was their business to go away. They saw Cory drop from the window, and they saw the fight. When Martineau went down, Cleo urged, "Oh, help him. Help him!"

Joe's training and years of service made it easy for him to remember and obey instructions. But this was something out of the ordinary. Also, his own nature impelled him. Added to this was the powerful effect of Cleo's plea. She was his lady, spurring him to knightly deeds. He ran forward and wrapped long arms around Cory, and pulled him off balance so that he could no longer strike at Martineau. Cory tried to break free, he tried to smash Joe's nose with the back of his head, he tried to hack his shins and stamp on his toes. None of these attempts was successful. There was nothing wrong with young P. C. Ainslie's reflexes.

Then Hearn dropped from the window, and Cassidy came running from behind the stand. Martineau rose groggily to his feet. Cory relaxed. "All right," he said. "What's all this about?"

"All right, kid. Scraper," Hearn whispered to Joe. He was younger than Joe, and junior to him. But he was his senior in the C.I.D. Joe released Cory and scarpered. And he had the sense to avoid going directly to Cleo. He tried to fade away into the crowd which had gathered a little distance away. Cleo was clearly visible in that crowd. It had arranged itself in line with her and behind her.

Cleo saw him coming, and moved a little way to meet him. There was nothing he could do but hold her by the arm and turn her around, and take her with him into the crowd. He saw curious, staring faces, and one of them he recognized. It was one of the three men who had sat at a table with Gerry Gee in his club, on Saturday night. He saw the man's eyes shift from himself to Cleo. On Saturday the man had seen Joe dancing with Cleo. He had seen her sitting at Joe's table after Olney had departed. Now, through Joe, he knew Cleo. That knowledge was evident in the sudden, cunning awareness of his glance. Joe silently cursed himself. He had been a fool, a disobedient fool, when he had gone to Martineau's assistance. Fool, fool, fool!

Meanwhile Cory was being hustled away. "Hold on a minute," he protested. "I've got a tenner on the next race, at three to one. If I'm not here to collect, I might never get it."

"I'll see you get it if you win," said Martineau. "What have you backed?"

"Number Two, The Dart."

"The first bookie, wasn't it? What's his name?"

"Abe Tyzack."

"He'll send you the money. What's your address?"

Cory opened his mouth to give his address, and changed his mind. "I don't want it sending to my address, if I'm not there," he said. "I'd never even get a sight of it."

Martineau immediately lost interest in Cory's bet. He had thought that it might serve to make the man reveal his address in time for a search of his room before the news of his arrest could come to the ears of his associates. "See to it, Cassidy," he said. "Take his ticket and collect his money if he wins."

Devery and Hearn took Cory away. Martineau went and sat in his own car, and waited for Cassidy. He needed time to get used to a certain idea before he talked to Cory again. Up and down the world there were men who could beat him in a fight. Of course he had known that, and he had known that someday he would meet one of those men. Tonight, after twenty-three years of the rough-and-tumble of police work, it had happened. And the man who had proved himself to be a better man than Martineau showed all the signs of being the dirtiest crook he had ever met. It was hard to accept.

FIFTEEN

AT HEADQUARTERS the stage was set in the bare, gray Interrogation Room. Cory was seated at the table in the middle of the room. Strong light poured down upon his dark, well-barbered head. Devery and Hearn were seated on hard wooden chairs near the door. The shorthand writer waited at his own small table.

Martineau entered and took his seat across the table from Cory. He looked at the man, and reflected that he had known perhaps a dozen like him, except that this was the only one who had ever been able to bring him to his knees. He looked at the man, and knew him. Pitiless, he thought. Intransigent. Without scruple. Without the pride which may keep a man honest, yet proud in his own perverse way. And of course a chronic Not Guilty character.

"Your winnings," he said, putting a little wad of five-pound notes on the table. "Did you know something?"

"Yeh. I knew it was going to win," Cory said with contempt. He picked up the money and put it into his pocket without counting it.

Martineau understood him perfectly. He was a wide boy. Wide boys were always contemptuous of policemen. The prisons

104

of England were full of contemptuous wide boys who had been put away for long stretches by patient policemen.

"You may as well put it back on the table, along with your other stuff," he said. "You needn't keep anything back, because you'll be properly searched when I've done talking to you."

Cory shrugged, and began to put the contents of his pockets on the table. Martineau picked up a wallet and inspected it with an air of boredom. He carefully refrained from looking at a glossy white packet of Players No. 3 and a shiny Colibri lighter. He knew that Cory could not be as cool as he looked. The room was warm, and Cory still wore his hat and raincoat. He had pushed the hat to the back of his head and unbuttoned the raincoat. Yes, he was warm. He would be sweaty enough to put good fingerprints on the cigarette packet and the lighter.

"What's your real name, Cory?" the policeman asked.

"Cory. Lewis Cory."

"What's your address?"

"Granchester."

"I want a more specific address than that."

"You won't get it."

"How long have you lived in Granchester?"

"Years."

"Where did you live before that?"

"Oh, here and there."

"In what part of Liverpool were you dragged up?"

The question did not disturb Cory. He said, "I was brought up proper. I'm no bastard copper."

"We're making inquiries about you in Liverpool. They'll give us your record."

Cory's glance moved then, to the packet of cigarettes. Martineau's hands were on the table. He cupped his left hand over the lighter, and with his right hand he picked up the cigarette packet, holding it daintily by the corners. He held it out at arm's length, and Devery came and took it. Then the sergeant came around and took the lighter.

"Take them to Sergeant Bird," said Martineau.

"You've no right to do that, I haven't been convicted yet," Cory said.

Martineau was amused, and his amusement held about the

same amount of contempt that Cory had displayed. He reflected that the man's remark was typical. The wide boy, himself un-hampered by any rule of conduct, was quick to tell an opponent what he could not do by right. Utterly dishonest himself, he would take advantage of all the laws made to protect honest men.

"I got your dabs under the Ways and Means Act," the police-man said. "What are you grumbling about? There's no ink on your fingers, is there?"

"I know what's right. I'll have a lawyer."

"You'll need one. But you haven't yet asked why you were brought here. Of course you know, don't you?"

"I neither know nor care. You've got nothing on me."

"We have enough, and we'll have more. I want you to realize that we'll be keeping you here. Do you want us to communicate with your wife?"

Cory shook his head. "That won't work, either. You don't know if I have a wife."

There was an interruption. It was Devery returning from his errand. He handed a note to Martineau. It was from Bird. "Ernest Rapp's fingerprints on both tire levers. On a spanner is the same thumbprint as on sheath."

The chief inspector put the note in his pocket, and studied the prisoner anew. He thought: A wide boy not wide enough to know that a shiny, slightly greasy tool would retain a fingerprint in still water. Cory's might be the dominant will and physique which held a gang of thieves together, but were his the brains which directed them? It was doubtful.

He turned to Devery. "Go and change the word on Ernie Rapp," he said. "Put it out to All Districts. He is now wanted on warrant, for murder. I'll see to the warrant when I've done with this fellow."

Devery departed. Martineau said to Cory, "Rapp will think you've shopped him."

"Rapp? Who's Rapp?" Cory demanded.

Martineau shook his head sadly, evincing a pity which he did not feel. "If only you knew what we've got on you and Rapp. Well, I won't show you the murder knife, and I won't show you the tools we found wrapped up in Webster Olney's clothes. It would only be a waste of time. I know you won't talk and I don't need you to talk. You won't say where you live or admit that you have a wife. Is there anybody who needs to be told that you've been locked up?"

Cory did not reply.

"How old are you?"

"I've forgot. I gave up counting birthdays."

"What do you do for a living?"

"I live on my investments."

"How long have you known Long Cue Lancaster?"

"Who's he?"

"He's an associate of Ernie Rapp, and Gerry Gee, and Arthur Beckett, and Jud Wragg, and yourself. There are six of you."

Cory was sarcastic. "Six of the best," he said.

Watching closely, Martineau thought that he detected covert relief. He had included Wragg's name with intent to deceive, and he thought that he had succeeded in his aim. Cory thought that the police were not seeking the sixth man, and that made him somewhat easier in his mind. Apparently the sixth man was the most important of all. In Cory's view, at any rate. And obviously that was because the sixth man was holding the loot from the Northern Steel job.

Well, there was no need to waste any more time with Cory. Martineau had expected no information from him, and had elicited a little. Now he could be taken down and charged, and locked up. He was in the bag, a dead pigeon.

That was what Martineau thought.

After the arrest of Lew Cory, Cleo hurried home to change her clothes, because Joe Ainslie forbade her to go to the Gee Gee Club in the coat she had worn at the dog track. He went home with her, and later to the club, but she suggested that she ought to enter the place alone. "There's no point in making it too obvious," she said.

Joe demurred. "I don't want to let you out of my sight. I think you were spotted. I'm sorry you ever got into this."

"I'm not sorry," Cleo retorted. "I'd do it again. Nobody will try to hurt me. At least they won't do it in the club."

On reflection, Joe was inclined to agree that Cleo would be

107

safe enough in the club. It would be later, on the way home, that she might be in danger.

"All right," he said. "But don't leave the place without letting me know." He put his hand in his pocket and produced a police whistle. "Take this, and if you need any help, blow it good and hearty."

Cleo took the whistle and went ahead. Joe waited until she was nearly out of sight, and then he followed. He entered the club, and found that he was the only member present. But the bar was open. He sat on a stool and discussed his earliness with the barman. "I didn't know," he said. "I won't come so soon again."

"We're always quiet of a Monday," the barman said as he supplied a gin-and-tonic. He was civil, but quite uninterested.

The members of the band appeared, and began to tune up and change reeds. Two girls came in, and then two more. They knew that Joe was Cleo's man, so they went to chat with the bandsmen. Gerry Gee arrived and, with a curious, surprised glance at Joe, he went through to the rear. After that there was a trickle of members and girls. One of the members was the man who had spotted Cleo. He looked quite startled when he saw Joe at the bar. Joe watched him, wondering if he would carry his news to Gerry Gee. He saw that the member was also watching. He looked away, and the man seized the opportunity to go through to the rear.

"There goes the bad news," Joe surmised. "If Gerry didn't know already, he knows now."

Two or three minutes later the member returned to the main room. His glance in Joe's direction was guarded. He joined two girls who were sitting at a table with a good view of the bar. "A grandstand seat," Joe said to himself. He felt sure that there would be some sort of trouble.

But there was no trouble. When Gerry appeared, he moved among the members in his usual way, and he spoke affably but casually to Joe. Things went on in a normal fashion. Eventually the first floor show started. It ran its course, and Cleo's performance was applauded by the man who had recognized her at the dog track. Still, Joe felt sure that the man had betrayed her to Gerry Gee.

After the show Cleo reappeared. She went to sit at a table with one of the girls. As soon as Joe could catch her eye, he beckoned her. She came to him. He rose and set a chair for her. They were at one of the outermost tables, near the wall.

"Has Gerry said anything?" he asked.

"Not about Cory. He came and told me he'd been able to find another dancer. He wouldn't be requiring me after tonight. I said that was all right with me. We parted friends, as you might say."

"I don't like it," Joe said.

"Don't like what?"

"I don't like this quietness. I'm sure Gerry knows I'm a policeman. He also knows you put the finger on Cory. But he says nothing and does nothing."

"He sacked me."

"You were leaving anyway. You'd told him you wanted out. I think he's planning some mischief. To you."

"Are you telling me *he's* in with Cory?"

"I am. That's strictly confidential."

Cleo thought about that. Then she said, "Wouldn't it be very risky for Cory's friends to try to attack me, when they know the police are protecting me? I'm sure they wouldn't take a big risk just to get their own back on me."

"Getting their own back is only part of it."

"Oh, I see. What happened to me would be a warning to others not to help the police or tell them anything."

"That's it. But we're going to see that nothing does happen to you. Have you much stuff to take away tonight?"

"There'll be two suitcases full of shoes and dresses and things."

"Pack them before the second cabaret. Then as soon as you've done your number, walk straight out by the back door without bothering to change. I'll be waiting with a taxi."

"From the rank in Chester Road? Sometimes there isn't a taxi on the rank around midnight. That's their busy time."

Joe pondered. The club's only telephone was in Gerry's office, and Gerry would certainly not permit Joe to use it. Would he allow Cleo to order a taxi? It would be natural for her to need one, to take her things away.

Gerry was sitting at a table a little distance away, talking to

109

three men. Joe looked at him. "Will his office be locked?" he asked. Cleo got the idea. "It isn't usually," she said. "I'll go and order the taxi now, for twelve-thirty."

She went, and returned too quickly to have succeeded in ordering a taxi. She went to Gerry's table, and spoke to him. He answered her quite good-humoredly, but she did not seem to be pleased with the answer. He seemed then to give her some sort of assurance which she had to accept. She returned to Joe.

"The office is locked. Gerry won't give me the key, but he says he'll order a taxi for me in a little while."

"And of course he'll forget," said Joe. "He'll forget on purpose, even if you remind him. I could go out and get a police car laid on, but the door would be closed against me when I came back. I don't want to leave you here alone."

"I don't want you to. Not now. I know Gerry. He's up to something."

"Right. Now, here's the drill. When you've finished your number, change as quickly as you can into street clothes. Leave your suitcases to be picked up tomorrow. I'll be watching that curtain. Come and show yourself for about half a second, and I'll join you. We'll try to get away before they're ready for us."

SIXTEEN

ONLY five minutes after Cleo had finished her last performance at the Gee Gee Club she signaled from the curtain that she was ready to go. Joe got up from his table. He had a hat and raincoat in the cloakroom, and he had decided that they could stay there for the night. He walked across the room to the bar, then along the front of it to where Jud Wragg was standing by the curtain. As he reached to open the curtain, Wragg put a hand on his shoulder.

"Hey, you can't go back there," he said.

Joe turned, and said, "Oh, sorry." As the hand dropped from his shoulder he caught it, and the arm too, and mistreated both with such sudden cruelty that poor Jud had to allow his body to move precipitately away from the curtain. His feet would have moved too, had not Joe's foot been in the way. Turning as he fell, he landed flat on his back on the dance floor, and slid a little way along the polished boards.

Joe passed through the curtain, and saw Cleo waiting for him at the head of the back stairs. He ran to her, and they hurried down the stairs. The back door was locked and barred, but it was a latch lock. He opened the door and looked out into the narrow, ill-lit street behind the club.

111

He spoke to Cleo in a rapid whisper as they moved away from the door. "I'm going to scout ahead, but I'll always have you in sight. Make for the cab rank. Walk fast, but don't run. And whatever happens don't stop unless I tell you to."

He ran across the street and began to move ahead of Cleo, on the opposite side. He could see into every doorway and around every corner before she reached it. She walked briskly, but quietly because she had not changed into high-heeled shoes.

Two minutes' walk brought the girl to the street she would have used if she had emerged from the club by the front door. It was a street of office buildings and small shops, not palatial but decent enough. Straight ahead, three hundred yards away, were the bright sodium lights of Chester Road, and round the corner in Chester Road was the taxi rank.

That three hundred yards looked like a mile to Joe as he flitted along the other side of the street. Except for Cleo, there was not a soul in sight and there was no sound at all. Between Cleo and Chester Road there were two cross streets.

Cleo walked on, to all appearances quite unconcerned. Ahead of her, Joe reached the last intersection. He stepped into a doorway two feet from the corner, and assured himself that all was clear on the girl's side of the road. He started to look cautiously round the corner on his side, and moved back quickly when he saw one sidelight and part of the radiator of a car. He was relieved to know that he could not have been seen by the occupants of the car. This looked like an ambush. The car had stopped on the wrong side of the road, so that it would be hidden by the corner until the last moment.

A slight suggestion of movement at the instant of perception gave him the impression that the car had rolled quietly to a stop precisely at that instant. The driver must have received the signal to move into position as soon as Joe revealed his intention to leave the club by the back door. He wondered how that had been done.

He stepped back into the doorway and made a quick calculation of possibilities. He was quite unarmed, with not even enough change in his pocket to make a weight for his fist. If there were more than two men in the car, the outlook was decidedly grim.

Cleo was drawing level, at the same brisk pace. She could see

Joe in the doorway, but she could not yet see the car. Then she came level, and she saw it. The car's engine did not start, but Joe heard a door opening. Cleo began to run. Then a running man flashed past Joe's corner, making for Cleo at top speed. He launched himself after the man, who was heavily built and obviously not a sprinter. He dived, and managed to get one fat ankle in both hands just as the foot was leaving the ground. The man seemed to be taken completely by surprise. He fell heavily, and sprawled his length on the pavement.

Joe released the ankle and rolled, half expecting to feel the boots of another assailant before he could get to his feet. He was conscious of a number of things almost, but not quite, simultaneously. There had been a tinkle of breaking glass—the acid bottle. Cleo was still running and was not far from Chester Road. The car was heading straight for him.

He leaped for the corner of the nearest building, and gained it as the car swept past along the sidewalk of the side street. He heard the end of its front bumper scrape along the wall before it veered away. He saw that the acid thrower had got to his feet and was starting a tottering run in the other direction. He went after him, assuming that he could easily catch him before the car could turn round.

The next moment he had changed direction and was running for his life. By some combination of the use of accelerator and brake, the car had been turned right around, with screaming tires, almost in its own length. This skidding operation was achieved on a dry road.

Joe reached his original doorway with a second to spare. He flattened there, protected by solid stone, and the car had to swerve away along the side street from which it had first emerged. He heard its squealing turn as he darted across the road again, intent on catching the acid thrower. It came after him again, and again he had to lose ground by taking refuge in a doorway while it swept past within inches of him. It went on, and stopped a little ahead of the limping fugitive. A door was flung open and the man fell into the car. It started again with the door hanging open.

Far away along the street the lights of an approaching car could be seen. The bluish blur of light above the windscreen was obviously a police sign. Joe saw the phenomenal skidding turn of the ambush car again. He started to run toward Chester Road, but took care to be in a doorway when the car drew near. When it had passed, he continued to run. He was thirty yards behind it when its driver recklessly cut the corner to turn along Chester Road.

The entire murderous incident had taken only a few seconds of time. Cleo had reached the corner and to her relief had found one taxi on the rank. She was telling the driver how he must take her back toward the Gee Gee Club to pick up her escort when the ambush car emerged precipitately into Chester Road. Unfortunately there was a big motor coach, without passengers, homing to its garage at high speed along the road. It passed the taxi rank and collided at an angle with the ambush car as it shot out into the road. There was a resounding clangor and a tearing of metal as the two vehicles locked. The coach dragged the car fifteen yards without shaking it off.

The pursuing police car stopped in time, and its two occupants alighted and ran to the scene of the accident. Joe also ran up. There was no need for any of them to run. Only one person involved in that accident could move, and that was the coach driver. He had reached to lower a near-side window and was angrily asking the other driver what the hell he was playing at. The diagonal impact had caused the car's passenger to be hurt the most. He was unconscious, and his face was already covered with blood. The driver was trapped in his seat and only able to make slight movements of his limbs.

When Cleo was safe home, Joe told the taxi driver to take him to the General Hospital. In the receiving ward he found a gathering of policemen and casualties. Martineau was there.

"Good, I wanted you," he said to Joe. "Tell me what happened."

Joe told him the full story. "Who was the driver of the car, sir?" he asked in conclusion.

"Long Cue Lancaster, and the fellow with him was Arthur Beckett. It looks as if we have enough on both of them to keep them for a long, long time."

"Are they badly injured?"

114

"Beckett has cuts, concussion and a broken leg. He stays here under guard. When they finally unwrapped Long Cue from around the steering column, he had contusions only. He goes into a cell tonight. The coach driver wasn't hurt, except for his feelings."

"How did they manage it, sir?"

"With the greatest of ease," Martineau answered with some bitterness. "Long Cue was already off the lead. Arturo slipped his when he left the café to go for his usual evening drink. We don't know how they arranged to meet."

"Can we do anything with Gee, sir?"

"It doesn't look like it. But we'll spare the others not at all. I want you to take a car and go and pick up the fragments of the acid bottle; any piece which is still holding a drop or two of liquid, nurse it carefully. Handle all big pieces by the edges. Put 'em on my desk."

"I'm glad it was no more than an attempt, sir."

"My word, so am I. But we'll make the most of it. This job is going to have more charges than the Battle of Balaclava."

At Headquarters Martineau talked to Long Cue Lancaster for only a little while before the man was locked up for the night. He was put in a cell with Cory, and the cell was "miked." It was an old dodge and one unlikely to succeed with those two, but it had to be tried. It was quite useless. Cory and Long Cue talked not at all in the night, and in the morning only about breakfast and the food Long Cue had had in other police cells.

Later Long Cue appeared before a magistrate, and only the charge of taking away a motorcar without the owner's permission was mentioned. The car had been taken from a private garage the night before, and obviously it had been one of those cases in which the thief knew where he could steal a car when he needed one. The police, represented at that stage by Chief Superintendent Clay, stated that there would be other charges. As in Cory's case, there was a remand in custody for four days, for further police inquiries.

Back again in a cell with Cory, Long Cue talked about cars and various kinds of motor racing. Cory listened and had little to say. With regard to dogs and horses he was rather more voluble, and definitely more knowledgeable than Long Cue. When the subject of women came up, both men spoke in the filthiest way, Long Cue with lip-smacking gusto and Cory with contempt. Though it could hardly be accepted as the whole truth, it did seem that neither man had ever had the slightest affection or respect for any woman.

The search for Ernie Rapp went on, but detectives could learn nothing of the man's movements. He had disappeared completely. Sergeant Bird announced that the fingerprint evidence involving Rapp and Cory was now conclusive: the prints on the sheath of the murder knife were his, and his prints were also on the spanner which had been found in the canal with Olney's clothes. The forensic laboratory confirmed the expectation that the blood which had been spilt in the Olney brake was of the same blood group as Olney's.

That was all, but there was a task which Martineau had not been able to do before. He went to the Olney Works and interviewed the employees. Because the murder had been committed on a Saturday evening, every man had a reasonable alibi. Every one of them had been out with somebody. Only the foreman had keys to the works. Martineau made a note of that. Every alibi would have to be checked, and the foreman's most carefully.

The chief inspector returned to Headquarters, thinking not about the foreman's keys, but about Webster Olney's. Those keys had never been found. Perhaps they never would be found. It was unlikely that Ernie Rapp still had them in his pocket, regardless of consequences though he was.

Back in his office, Martineau found that Lew Cory's record had arrived from Liverpool. It was the first reply to Bird's letters, with Cory's prints, to Scotland Yard, Wakefield, and the suspect's probable home town. The man's real name was Lewis Corrigan, and the record was long and nasty. He had been a pimp and a prostitutes' bully. There were three convictions for the offense which the Americans call "the badger game," which in certain British circles is called "bugging." Usually, too, he had made use of his ability to intimidate or thrash his victims, whether they were men or women.

"One of those," Martineau muttered. "My word, this lot is a real shower."

SEVENTEEN

THE OTHER SIDE

BEN OLNEY, sleeping none too soundly, was brought to tense wakefulness by a sound near the window of his room. Through the thin curtains, in silhouette against street lighting, he saw the foot and ankle, then the hand and arm, of a man. It seemed that someone had climbed the fall pipe to a point eighteen inches from his window, and was now stepping onto the sill.

Ben slipped out of bed. As he did so the man stepped wholly onto the sill and crouched awkwardly to open the window wider. Ben crept to the side of the window. He took up a position from which he could strike with his right fist at an intruded head. But the man on the sill did not intrude his head. He parted the curtains a little way and uttered a cautious hiss. Then he whispered, "You there, Olney? It's me, Ernie."

Ben drew back the curtains farther, and the small, wiry figure of Rapp slipped into the room.

"What the hell have you come here for?" Ben demanded, muted but indignant.

Rapp turned and rearranged the curtain. "I wanted to see you," he replied calmly.

"You'll bring the cops here."

"Cool down," the little man said. "There's no copper any-where near here, an' none near your works. I been watchin' both places for long enough. I wanted to know if they was on to you yet."

Ben was somewhat mollified. "And they're not?"

"No. They'll never think of you. You're safe."

"What was it you wanted?"

"I want my money out."

"You can't have it. It was agreed there was to be nobody paid out except by a majority decision. There's got to be four of us."

"You're batty. How can there be four of us when three of us is in the nick? You think I can wait forever?"

"What's your hurry? Are you hard up?"

"Not more nor usual. I want to be on my way. I've got a boat. A feller's goin' to see me safe in Cape Town for five hundred quid."

"That's no place to go. It's a foreign country now."

"Don't argue. They talk English, don't they?"

"When does the boat sail?"

"That's my business. Just give me the money. I want to have it ready."

"Well, you can't have it tonight. I don't know when you can have it. At the moment it's too hot to touch."

"Give me my money or I'll slit your gut!"

"Belt up!" Ben retorted. "If you start any bother here, you'll *never* see your money." He was not physically afraid, but he was shaken by the knowledge that this savage little animal could ruin everything by trying to carry out his threat. He moved to the bedside table and groped for his cigarettes. "Here, *you* cool down," he said. "Have a cig."

They sat on the bed and smoked in the darkness. "I'll help you if I can, you know that," Ben said. "But I've got to be care-ful. I'm responsible for that money. The others are expecting me to keep it safe for them."

Rapp was silent. Something in his attitude, and in the way he breathed, revealed that he was thinking hard.

At last he spoke. "What about Lew?" he asked. "Will you keep his money safe after they've stretched his neck?"

Ben thought about that. He had thought about it before. He

118

remained in doubt. So long as Cory had no grudge against his accomplices, no feeling that they had failed him in any way, he would go in silence to the gallows. He would not give the police the satisfaction of recovering the Northern Steel money. But if he thought that he had been betrayed, at the last moment he would take his revenge. And in that lay the cause of doubt. Who knew what was in Cory's mind at that moment? Was he thinking that the son of a murdered man had given his name to the police?

"That's a problem," Ben admitted. "We couldn't even give the money to his widow, if he has one. Too dangerous."

"Come off it," was Rapp's scoffing whisper. "You wouldn't even think of it."

Ben perceived the trend of Rapp's reflections. If Rapp did not escape from the country, sooner or later he would be arrested. With Cory, and possibly with Long Cue also, he would be tried for murder. He might be convicted, and ultimately hanged. He thought that Ben was viewing the prospect with satisfaction. He assumed that Ben was hoping to have a larger share of the plunder.

"Don't get any wrong ideas," Ben said. "Same as anybody else, I like money. But I like to be safe, too. I'd be glad to see you get away with your share. I'd feel a lot safer. I'd be glad to see Cory and Long Cue out of the country, too. It'd mean a lot less worry for me."

"I could get Lew on that boat with me," Rapp whispered thoughtfully. "Long Cue an' all, happen. It'd be company for me. They couldn't so well knock three of us on the head an' shove us over the side."

"There's only one thing wrong with that idea. Cory and Long Cue are in a cell."

"They can be got out. Then we can have our divvy, and scarper."

"Get 'em out of police cells?"

"Yers. Easy. I know the setup. By God I ought to. All we need is a glass cutter, a couple good hacksaws, an' a drop of oil to make a quiet job of it."

"Suppose some bobby comes strolling by while we're busy on the bars?"

"No bobby 'ull come. The cell windows are in the police station yard. In the middle of the night the yard is as quiet as the grave. That's a fact, an' I'm the man who knows it."

"When do you reckon we can do this job?"

"Now. Tonight. It's a fine night."

"And where will we take them?"

"I know a place."

Ben thought about it. He tried to think the matter through, weighing all the chances. It was much too late to roam the streets looking for a car to steal so one of the Olney vehicles would have to be used. Well, an Olney vehicle had been used before, and the police did not suspect Ben. It was a risky business altogether; audacious. *Toujours de l'audace,* as the fellow said. The advantages of success were great. Three satisfied customers. They would trust him henceforth—as far as they could trust any man—and he could give them their money and let them go to hell in their own ways. If they were arrested subsequently they would take their punishment in silence. And they would be off Ben's hands, out of his life. He would not have to worry about them any more. He would have to forget all his half-formed ideas about avenging his father, but no doubt life would take its revenge on those three.

"Have you gone yellow on me?" Rapp gritted.

"No. I was just figuring it out."

"Figurin' hell. Go on, get dressed."

EIGHTEEN

ALL DAY Tuesday, and Tuesday night, Cory and Long Cue again shared the same cell, and not at any time did they make an utterance which could be of use to the police. They were quiet prisoners, old hands who knew that there was neither profit nor comfort to be obtained by bad behavior. Nevertheless, the jailer was to look in at them every hour, because it was understood that they were rather special prisoners.

The jailer on Nights looked at them at four o'clock in the morning, but at five o'clock he did not take the trouble. But at a quarter to six he went to see that all was well before he handed over his keys to the Early Turn jailer. He saw two empty cots. Messieurs Cory and Lancaster had arisen, and departed.

Martineau was informed. He rolled wearily out of bed and came down to see for himself, and when he had seen he swore. Obviously the two prisoners had been helped to escape by someone outside. The windows of the cells were in the police station yard, and it had been thought that this made them all the more secure. Now it could be seen that hadn't been so. In the daytime and evening the station yard was a place for leaving cars or for waiting with them. At such times there were never fewer than half a dozen vehicles in the yard, and usually as many police officers. But after midnight, when the streets were deserted, personnel with cars did not bother to put them in the yard. As the night wore on, policemen used the yard less and less frequently. From two o'clock until six in the morning, when even a big police station is quiet, the yard was a place for complete solitude. The man who had rescued the prisoners had had plenty of time to work on a cell window. He had only needed to be noiseless, and that, apparently, he had been.

The two thick steel bars of the cell window had been severed with a hacksaw, and the thick glass had been cut with a diamond. The windows were eight feet above the ground on the outside, and seven feet above the floor on the inside. The operation from inside was easily understood. Long Cue could help Cory to climb out, and then pull himself up.

Well, two desperate and vengeful men had succeeded in getting away. Martineau realized that Cleo Patton was at that moment unguarded and he sent men to watch the front and back of the house where she lived. It was not probable that two men on the run would consider immediate revenge, but it was possible.

At first it was not understood how the window had been reached from outside. There was no ladder in the yard, and no box or bin which a man could have used as a platform. The P.C. who had been Nights on that area had not gone home to bed like his mates. Though the escape had been made from a police station, it had been an occurrence on his beat, and he had stayed to give what help he could. He was questioned. Had he noticed anything, anything at all? There was something. He had seen a pickup truck not far from the station, going toward it, just before three o'clock. The gate of the station yard was never closed. The driver of the truck could have chosen his moment to drive quietly into the yard and stop underneath the cell window. The truck itself could have been the platform from which he worked on the bars. When the job was done, there had been transport to some hiding place. The escapers had been saved the perilous ordeal of sneaking afoot along empty streets.

"He had his nerve," Martineau growled. "How did he know which cell they were in?"

That was a question which could only be answered with a

guess. There were ten cell windows in a row. The prisoners had had no matches or lighter by which they could have showed a glimmer through the thick glass. The rescuer must have tapped cautiously on each window until he received a reply. He had had luck on his side. As it happened, all the other prisoners were drunks who would be sleeping heavily. He had been able to rouse his friends without rousing anyone else.

Martineau did not accept the reports of observers as gospel. They could be fooled, they could be mistaken, or they could—though it rarely happened in a serious case—be scamping the job and covering up on paper. Nevertheless, it was reasonable to assume that Gerry Gee was not the rescuer. Could Dixie Costello have got them out in order to make them answer his questions? That was possible, but doubtful. It was more likely to have been Rapp, if he knew where to find transport. Or the unknown sixth man could have emerged from safe obscurity to do the job.

Where could Rapp have found a pickup truck? He was not a motor criminal at all, and it was even possible that he was unable to drive. If he still had the keys of the Olney Works he could have borrowed the truck from there. Martineau decided to make inquiries about that.

He went to his office and set on foot every possible operation which would result in the capture of the fugitives. The press, the BBC, and independent television people were given the news. Policemen all over the country were alerted. Detectives prepared to visit the homes and haunts of all known criminals in the city. Inquiries were arranged with a view to discovering if any person had suddenly begun to buy more than his or her usual quantities of meat, groceries, cigarettes or liquor.

The Northern Steel Corporation's reward for information had finally been announced, and the public guesses of newspapermen had made sure that everyone knew of the possible connection between the Olney job and the Barton job, and the Northern Steel robbery. If the fugitives were running, each with his share of the loot, some wayfarer would see them. If they were hiding in the city, some dog-nosed informer would smell them out. If local informers were afraid to speak, the police themselves would eventually track them down.

Soon after nine o'clock that morning Martineau visited the

Olney Works. Sergeant Bird went also, driving his van with its load of equipment. At that time the cabinet works was a scene of activity, and the roar of saws and other woodworking machines was a pervading noise. Ben Olney was in his little office, dictating replies to the morning's mail. The woman who was taking the dictation looked sensible, efficient, and fifty.

There was some irritation in Ben's reply to Martineau's greeting. He must have been aware of it himself, because he immediately said, "Sorry, inspector. You've just caught me at a busy time. What can I do for you?"

"Who was the first to arrive here this morning?" the policeman wanted to know.

"I was. I always am."

"Was everything in order?"

"Yes, as far as I know."

"You told me you didn't keep a record of mileage for the brake. Do you keep a record of the pickup truck?"

"Yes, it's in the garage."

"Perhaps I'd better take a look at it," Martineau said.

In the garage two men in shirt sleeves were cleaning funeral cars. The lorry was out somewhere, but the pickup truck was in its place. Ben went to the bench near the door and took a grubby copybook from a drawer. He found the pages devoted to the truck and read out the mileage figure. Martineau looked at the speedometer. The figure was correct to the tenth of a mile which Ben had quoted.

"Who made the entry?" Martineau asked.

"Our foreman. He used the truck yesterday afternoon, to take some window frames to an outside job."

"He just got back at five o'clock," one of the car cleaners volunteered. "He was the last man to use the truck yesterday, so he entered the mileage."

"You saw him make the entry?" Martineau asked.

"Yes, I did." The man replied positively.

"Did you see what he had written?"

"No. I just saw him look at the speedometer and write something in the book."

Martineau took the book from Ben and studied the entry. It was in pencil like all the other entries, and it seemed to be perfectly in order. Well, ultraviolet rays would show if there had been an erasure and an alteration.

"Mind if I borrow this for a few hours?" he asked.

"Take it," Ben replied without hesitation. "I'd just like to have it back here for five o'clock if you can manage it."

Martineau nodded. He tucked the book under his arm and turned to look at Bird, who was working on the platform and sides of the truck with a magnet. "Are you finding anything?" he asked.

"Plenty," the busy sergeant replied.

Martineau went to look, and saw steel filings on the magnet. Ben, who had followed him, also saw the filings.

"Iron filings," he commented. "That's funny. We don't do anything with iron. What is all this about the truck?"

"I may be able to tell you later. Just now I'd like to make sure the speedometer is in order."

"George," Ben said to one of the men. "You heard the inspector. See if it's all right."

The man came and stooped to his task, and ten seconds later he made his report. "It's been disconnected," he said. "Somebody's been messing about with it."

"Here's your book," said Martineau. "I won't need it."

He left Bird working on the truck, looking for fingerprints now, and went out into the yard. He asked Ben to send the foreman out to him. The man came. He was questioned about the previous night. He said he had been where any honest man should have been, in bed with his wife.

Martineau nodded and sent the man back to his work. He did not even think of Ben's keys, or of Ben who had presumably been sleeping alone. He went away believing that Webster Olney's keys were still available to Ernie Rapp and the one member of the gang whose name was not yet known.

NINETEEN

JOE AINSLIE spent only part of his working days as escort to Cleo Patton. He picked her up at her flat that afternoon and went with her to the little dress shop in Mere Street, and waited about while she talked business with a sweet old lady. Then he took her back to the flat again. She made a meal for both of them, saying that she would like to see how much a full-sized policeman could eat. The food was good, and she was duly impressed by his appetite. An hour after the meal was spent in a discussion which was delicious to both of them. It was about marriage. Joe attacked the subject vigorously and Cleo resorted to laughing evasion. When he became physically demonstrative, she found that the flat was not big enough for evasion, and she reminded him that he had planned to be back at Headquarters by eight o'clock to see if anything had been happening there.

"You know very well Mr. Martineau is depending on you to solve the case," she said with a twinkle as she straightened his tie. "Go and do your duty."

He departed reluctantly, and in the street he discovered that a fine rain was falling. This reminded him that his hat and raincoat were still in the cloakroom at the Gee Gee Club. The time was half past seven. He had time to go and get them.

Whether or not Gerry Gee was still annoyed with him, Joe did not want to go into the club. He would simply go to Tony Young at the reception counter and ask for his hat and coat. Two minutes of a job.

But when he entered the foyer of the club he saw that both Tony Young and Jud Wragg were there. The big man straightened when he saw who had entered. His red face grew redder, but he said quietly, "I'll give you time to take your coat off if you don't want to ruin that suit."

Joe kept his distance, and was watchful. But he said, "I'm sorry I had to do that the other night. I took you by surprise. But I had to do it. I couldn't afford a second's delay."

"You can afford it now."

"I can't. As a police officer I can't indulge in rowdyism. If you want a turn, we'll have to go into the police gymnasium. I don't want to do it, but I'll admit I owe it to you."

"Forget it, Jud," said Tony Young. "He's apologized. First time I've ever heard a copper apologize for belting somebody. Shake hands and forget it."

"He made a fool of me in front of everybody," Jud growled.

"I'm sorry, I had it to do, as you must know by now. If I hadn't managed to get out of there quickly, Cleo would have got acid in her face."

Tony nudged Jud. "There you are," he murmured. "You know what we were talking about. We've got to find out something about this." He went and took a cautious look into the clubroom. "All clear," he said. "Now shake on it and go and bring the lad a drink. He can have it here."

Jud offered his hand, and Joe took it. But he said, "I don't want a drink. All I want is my hat and coat."

"Well, have a cigarette," said Tony hospitably. "I'll get your coat in a minute."

It was obvious that Tony wanted to talk. Of course he wanted information. In getting it, he might also provide some.

"Give me my coat, and then we'll talk," Joe insisted. "I want to be able to walk out if Gerry shows up and starts giving his lip."

"Fair enough," said Tony. He brought the hat and coat. Joe put the coat over his arm and left the hat within reach on the counter. He accepted a cigarette from Tony. Jud moved to a spot from which he could listen to the conversation and watch the clubroom at the same time.

"Me and Jud have a stake in this place," Tony explained. "We don't believe in anything illegal. Gerry worked a fast operation on Verney Barton. If he does down, we'll have to run the club. But he thinks he's going to get away with it."

"I can't tell you anything," Joe said.

"You can give your private opinion."

"I can give you some advice. Get ready to run the club for a long time. And don't quote me to anybody."

Tony smiled. "Fair enough. There's more than Verney's business, isn't there? Bobbies in the club, Webster Olney rubbed out. Are they just watching the place because Olney was a member or is there more to it?"

"No comment."

"Well, they're seeking Lew Cory and this fellow Rapp for murder. They aren't seeking Gerry, are they? He's right here. So it doesn't look as if he's in it, does it?"

"Agreed. It doesn't look so."

"So what's it all about, then? Is it right Olney was somehow mixed up with that payroll robbery?"

"Again, no comment," said Joe, and then there was an interruption. Four men marched in by the front door. The big man who appeared to be the leader had an air of confident equanimity.

"Police," he said briskly. "Search and checkup."

Tony Young was outraged. "Are you trying to ruin us altogether? Where's your warrant?"

The man produced an important-looking document, slapped the palm of his hand with it, and put it back in his pocket. "Are you Gerry Gee?" he asked.

"No. He's in his office. Let me see that warrant."

"I'll show it to Gee. Lead me to him. I want to see the list of members."

"What for? Martineau has it."

"Martineau can keep it. He's been superseded. I'm Superintendent Langley of New Scotland Yard. Now take me to the office."

Tony went away with the four men. They had been followed

into the club by two more groups of four, making a dozen detectives in all. *If* they were detectives. Joe Ainslie was quickly coming to a conclusion about that. Granchester City was a big force whose chief constable had never been known to call in Scotland Yard.

Besides, every one of the twelve men was a stranger to Joe. The Yard did not send out teams of twelve. If they were genuine policemen, at least ten of them were members of his own force. The appearance together of ten colleagues, all completely unknown to him, was a coincidence he would not accept.

Five of the remaining eight men went on into the club. Three men remained at the door. Joe picked up his hat. "Ah, well," he said to Jud Wragg. "I'd better be going."

"Nobody goes out," said one of the three men, and he certainly had an air of authority. "Members can come in, but nobody leaves without permission."

Joe had expected some statement of that sort and had already decided that there was nothing to be gained by waiting for a better chance. He lurched away from the counter, and with a swift backhanded blow he wiped the brim of his hat across the man's eyes. Almost at the same time he slung his raincoat at a second man, and then he charged the third man, who was between him and the door.

He did not succeed in getting away. The third man was not taken by surprise. He was thickset and immovable. Joe failed to get by him, and had to fight him. Soon he was attacked from behind by the other two, and he received blows which dazed and weakened him. Then, miraculously, he was fighting one man only, and soon he had an ally who came in from the side and put the man down with a mighty blow with a rubber truncheon. The ally was Jud Wragg, who had been quick to realize that the intruders could not be policemen because one of them was using a knuckle-duster. He had reached for the truncheon, which was kept under the reception counter, and laid the men out one-two-three.

Others would be coming, to see what the disturbance was about. "Run, Jud, they'll murder you," Joe said. He ran out of the club, with Jud at his heels. There was no guard outside. The two men ran out of the yard, and when they perceived that there was no pursuit they eased their pace to a jog trot.

"Not real coppers?" Jud wanted to know.

"Bogus," Joe replied. "Where's nearest phone?"

"Trinidad Inn, round the corner. I'll show you."

They trotted on. "Bogus bogeys," Jud breathed happily. "I showed 'em. I oughter get a medal."

Martineau was surprised but not amazed by P. C. Ainslie's message. It was no rare occurrence for crooks to pose as policemen, but never before had he known them do it in such numbers. He did not immediately see the reason for the imposture nor did he pause to think about it. He immediately telephoned the divisional duty inspector.

"Hargreaves here," the inspector said.

"Martineau. Do you know anything about a raid on the Gee Gee Club?"

"No. Who's running it? I should have been informed."

"This is strictly unofficial. Twelve men—twelve, I said—reckoning to be bobbies in plain clothes. They're in the club at this moment. Their leader calls himself Superintendent Langley of New Scotland Yard."

"Oh, he does, does he?" Hargreaves growled. "Right, I'll see to it."

Martineau went along to see the sights, and he took Devery, Cassidy and Hearn with him in case there was anything for his department to do. As he got out of his car not far from the club he was met by Ainslie and Jud Wragg. He eyed the rubber truncheon which Wragg still held in his hand.

"Property of the club, sir," Ainslie said. "But for Mr. Wragg's help, I might never have got away."

"Very good," said Martineau. "Don't forget to mention it in your report."

The men in plain clothes watched the men in blue enter the club. They followed. The second—real—police raid was a complete success. Apparently the bogus detectives had assumed that Ainslie and Wragg were only a member and a staff member who had not wanted to be questioned by the police. That being the case, they had not expected the real police to be called.

In the club, the imitation detectives were greatly outnumbered. They were meekly surrendering to the men in uniform. Hargreaves was counting prisoners. Ainslie said to Martineau, "The leader isn't here, sir. He might be in Gee's office."

The chief inspector nodded, and took his following through to the office. The door was locked. He did not trouble to knock, but charged with the effectiveness of long practice. The door flew open and revealed a scene of suffering. Gerry Gee had been stripped naked and tied to a chair. He was the sufferer, with half a dozen really bad-looking burns on his abdomen. A man with a lighted cigar was lounging on a corner of the desk, and evidently he was the torturer. He had ended the torture or was giving himself or his victim a respite. There were no other people present.

Gerry looked very ill indeed. His face was dead-white and there were marks around his mouth where tape had been applied. The tape lay on the desk. Apparently he had been gagged to prevent him from screaming, with the instruction to nod his head when he was ready to give information. Whether he had given it or been about to give it was a matter to be ascertained. Certainly he had taken a lot of punishment before he had weakened. He was undoubtedly of tougher fiber than Martineau had supposed.

The man with the cigar was the fraudulent Scotland Yard man. When Martineau and his men entered the room, he looked round coolly, and carefully placed the smoldering weed on the desk's big ashtray.

"Police?" he asked. "I'm glad you came. I was about to release this poor man."

"I can see you were," Martineau said. There were moments when he believed that policemen ought to be allowed to inflict corporal punishment on the spot. This was one of the moments. His blow knocked the man off his perch and stretched him on the floor.

"Sergeant," he snapped. "Put the bangles on this lump of cat's meat, and take it to the lockup."

TWENTY

Doctored, bandaged and clothed, and sitting at his desk, Gerry Gee looked much better than when Martineau had seen him tied to a chair.

"I can't help you," he said. "It was just as the man said. The fellow who was burning me bolted when he came in."

"That's so ridiculous it isn't even worth talking about, but it looks as if we'll have to," the chief inspector retorted. "If anybody else had done that, he couldn't have got away. Those fellows had the place covered back and front when our men arrived and took over."

"Well, he did get away."

"If you utter that statement in the witness box, you'll be indicted for perjury. We're taking statements from the staff. They'll tell the truth in his case. Tony Young has already told me he had to bring the leader here, and he had to leave you here with that man and two more. It's perfectly clear what happened. You had to be questioned in private. As soon as you were tied up, the boss mobster cleared the others out. Then he started to put the pressure on. He was the one who scorched your belly for you."

"He didn't," said Gerry stubbornly. "It was none of that mob who burned me."

132

"You're scared of a shower of imported tearaways from Birmingham, or maybe London. Or perhaps you're scared of the man who imported 'em. But you'll tell the truth or else. Did the cigar boy get to know what he wanted?"

"I don't know what you're talking about."

"Well, you weren't burned for nothing, were you?"

"It was a grudge job, according to the chap who did it. I think he was somebody with delusions. Loopy."

"Oh, come off it. The cigar smoker was after the Northern Steel money. Our men found half a dozen of his mob systematically searching the premises while he was working on you. A certain man in this town has got the griff that you were mixed up in the Northern Steel do. He was trying to get at the loot through you. There's only one man I know who has enough influence to bring in a complete commando from out of town. We both know who he is."

Gerry shook his head. "You're mistaken about me."

"Like hell I am. That lot are Brummagem Boys by the sound of them, and there's an experienced officer on his way from there right now. He should be able to identify a few of 'em. At least we'll get their records."

Gerry shrugged. "They'll never spill anything."

"That is so. They're like you. They're gangsters. You know what this means, don't you?"

"How can I know? It's all a mystery to me."

"Well, I'll tell you. A certain man has incurred some expenses tonight. Fairly heavy expenses, I should think. Unless you spilled what you knew—and I think you were about to, but didn't— he's got no return for his money. He won't like that. He'll never let you or any of your accomplices alone till he's got his hands on that money."

Again Gerry shrugged. "*I* don't know where the money is."

"He might have another go at you."

"I'll make damn sure nobody gets at me again."

"He might set the Dog on you."

Gerry could not hide his dislike of that possibility, but he made no reply. Martineau looked at him in silent frustration. He had been unable to prevent him from being released on bail for the Barton break-in. He could not take him into protective custody or arrest him as a material witness, as an American police officer might have done. He was not allowed to tap his telephone or mike his office. He could not and would not fake a charge to hold the man. Having only knowledge and no evidence of his complicity in other crimes, he had to leave him at liberty. Moreover, everything he did to him or said to him would eventually come under the close scrutiny of an alert counsel for the defense. As a policeman—and somewhat prejudiced in favor of his own profession—he was of the opinion that the careful British legal system provided too many safeguards for criminals and not enough help to the police.

He sighed. He had even been unable to have Gerry detained in hospital. The club owner had insisted on leaving. Martineau knew why. Gerry wanted to warn his friends in hiding that Dixie Costello had joined the game in earnest. Those men would fear Costello more than they feared the police.

As he left Gerry, Martineau realized that it would be worse than useless to interview Costello. That alert character would blandly deny everything and would in those circumstances succeed in getting more information than he gave. It would be just as futile as the routine interrogation of the Birmingham mobsters now being conducted by subordinates at Headquarters. A dozen interviews would produce a dozen sheets of questions with flippant replies.

The chief inspector returned wearily to Headquarters. All day he had been obliged to occupy himself with routine matters while oppressed by a feeling that time was running out. After the visit to the Olney Works he had had to interview Arthur Beckett in hospital. Routine had demanded it, and it had been a waste of time. Later the chief constable had decided to have a conference at which a number of opinions had been expressed by senior officers. None of the opinions had given Martineau any new ideas. He had squirmed with impatience, but even he had not had the nerve to tell the chief and his assembled staff that he was too busy to talk to them.

He had escaped from the conference only because he had had to attend the inquest on Webster Olney. It would have been no use trying to hurry the coroner. It had been six o'clock, with only an hour of daylight left, when he had been free to return to the direction of the hunt for Cory, Lancaster and Rapp. He had barely finished making new dispositions in that pursuit when Joe Ainslie had rung in with his news of the bogus police raid on the Gee Gee Club.

Now, being hungry and thirsty, he sent for tea and sandwiches, and fell into meditation upon certain questions which had been asked at Olney's inquest. The questions had been pertinent, and unanswerable. A murder had been solved, but the motive for murder was still obscure. The motive might have seemed clear if Olney had happened to blunder on to the scene of some criminal act or its preparation. But he had been deliberately lured to the spot where he had been killed. Had he been lured with murder in mind or for some other purpose, some purpose which had proved to be futile or abortive? Had he been in league with the men who stole the Northern Steel payroll? Had he been the one with special knowledge who had directed the disposal of Verney Barton's body?

"He was a bit old for that sort of lark," Martineau decided. "But he certainly had the knowledge."

He thought of all the old criminals he had known. Fences, swindlers, thieves. Old, but greedy and pitiless. Capable of murder themselves, some of them. Brainy and experienced, others. He had known several elderly men who would have been quite capable of supervising the activities of Cory, Rapp and Company. Olney could not be ruled out merely on account of age.

So Olney could have been a member of the gang, though probably not an active member in a physical sense. He could have been the treasurer. Why, then, had he been killed? Martineau could think of a number of reasons. He could have been killed in cold blood for his share of the money, or because he was distrusted for some reason, or because it was feared that he would not be able to stand up to police questioning in a murder case. He could have been killed in a rage by someone like Rapp or Long Cue because he had refused a request. It could have been a request to be given money while it was yet too hot to handle, a request which any one of the gang was quite capable of making. Well, he had been killed, and quite possibly the money had been moved from the place where he had hidden it.

That was one aspect of the case. There was another. Olney

could have been an honest man who was killed because he knew something. About Gerry Gee? Something which he had seen or overheard at the club? Could he have known what Verney Barton had known? The two men had not been close friends, but they had been well acquainted.

If Olney's dangerous knowledge had not been concerned with Gee, could it have been something to do with Ben or that foreman Quaint, Luther Quaint? Ben seemed to be all right. It was unlikely that he would set the scene for the murder of his own father but it was not impossible. The foreman seemed to be all right too, but he was a more likely suspect than Ben.

Martineau looked at his watch. He sighed, because he was tired. He would have a go at Ben and his foreman in the morning. He would give them the works, even if only for the purpose of eliminating them as suspects. He hoped that he could get away home in reasonable time, not later than midnight at any rate. In the morning he would be rested, and ready for the fray.

The telephone rang.

The call was from C Division, and Martineau realized that it was the first result of Gerry Gee's freedom to use a telephone. At half past ten a constable on his beat had found that there had been a break-in at the Drill Hall, Churlham. It was thought that entry had been obtained by picking the big old-fashioned lock of an outer door. Inside, the armory had a door with a modern lock. The door had been broken open by the use of several crowbars or large jemmies. It had been a rough job and possibly a noisy one, but it had been quick.

Churlham Drill Hall was the depot of a Territorial infantry battalion, and it was in an outer division of the city police. Normally the break-in would have been none of Martineau's business. On this occasion he made it his business. He had been afraid that something like this might happen.

He reached the Drill Hall at the same time as the first Army man to arrive. This was a young fellow with the rank of captain, who spent his days helping his father to run a chocolate factory and many of his evenings and weekends commanding a company. The captain was naturally concerned about the break-in, but he was indignant in one respect only.

"I knew there'd be more trouble with that bladdy old lock," he declared. "Only six months ago some johnny got into the mess an' pinched all the bladdy gin."

"Are you the adjutant?" Martineau asked.

"No, the old aj is away. I'm very temp'rary."

"Are you familiar with the contents of the armory?"

"I suppose so, though I don't know just how much of everything we have. It's all in the book, though."

They entered the armory. "We don't have the latest weapons here, you know," the captain said. His glance came to rest on a rack of submachine guns. "Three T.S.M.G.'s missing, for a start."

"Tommy guns?" Martineau was perturbed. "That's bad. That's very bad."

"It doesn't look like the jolly old I.R.A.," the captain said. "They'd have taken a lorryload."

"I agree with you. We haven't had I.R.A. trouble for years, anyway. Can you see what else is missing?"

The captain stepped into another room and looked along rows of chained and racked rifles. The display was so orderly that one missing rifle would have been conspicuous by its absence. He returned and opened a shallow cupboard. "This should be locked," he said.

"It's been forced," said Martineau. "How many things are missing?"

In the cupboard, shining in oily cleanliness, service revolvers rested in rows. There were gaps in the rows.

"I'm not sure," the captain said. "Three or four."

"Ammunition?" Martineau asked.

The young man went to a bank of labeled drawers. Some of the drawers had been forced. "Yes," he said. "They've got ammo."

"Hand grenades?"

The captain went to an unlabeled drawer. It was secure. "If they've taken grenades, they won't be any good," he said. "All the detonators are in here."

137

"Well, that's something, at any rate," Martineau said. He turned to the divisional detective inspector. "It's all yours, Mather," he said. "I expect you'll have your own ideas about it."

"My ideas will be the same as yours, sir, after that do tonight."

Martineau nodded and departed, having no further interest in the Drill Hall break-in. It was enough for him to know that criminals in his bailiwick were now in possession of weapons with deadly fire power. Thompson submachine guns! One each for Cory, Rapp and Lancaster. This was their reaction to a raid on the Gee Gee Club instigated by Dixie Costello. They were prepared to meet the new threat to the Northern Steel loot with bullets. Would they also be ready to use their Tommy guns against the police, to resist arrest? Of course they would. They hated policemen. Long Cue Lancaster's attempt to murder P. C. Ainslie with that lethal weapon a motorcar was an indication of his frame of mind. His friends would be no less murderous.

As he drove back toward the center of the city Martineau thought about Dixie Costello with grim humor. It would have given him much pleasure to allow that ulcer on the community's stomach to lead his crowd of antisocial pests into a hail of bullets. Of course he knew that he could not do it. It was a great pity.

It was one o'clock in the morning when he arrived at Costello's flat. It was a big flat above an expensive restaurant which was also his property. The boss mobster's white Rolls-Royce was standing at the curb. He was still up and about, apparently, though no music or other party sounds could be heard.

Dixie was probably having a small, private party with one red-haired girl. All his personal cars were white and all his girls were redheads. He changed models frequently.

Martineau rang the bell at the discreet private entrance next door to the restaurant. He waited, and heard a window being opened. Dixie called "Who's there?" without showing himself.

"Police," was the reply.

"That sounds like a dear, dear friend of mine," came Dixie's voice, in deep disgust. He showed himself at the window. "What in hell do you want at this time?"

"I want to talk to you for your own good."

"Never! Impossible! Come back in the morning."

"I'm too busy to waste two journeys on you. You'll see me now or you'll regret it."

"Well, well. Drama. You'd better come up."

There was the slightest of clicks. Martineau pushed the door and it swung open. He climbed the stairs and found Dixie waiting for him, holding open the door of the flat.

He looked at the boss mobster and saw a man of his own age, of medium height but compact and powerful. His strong, rather handsome face had an outdoor complexion which was certainly not due to the wind on the heath. Dixie's healthy coloring was an excellent advertisement for Scotch whisky.

"I hope you won't be staying long," he said with humorous rudeness.

"Five minutes, unless you want a long chat," said Martineau. He entered a room furnished with casual disregard for expense, and encountered a redolence of cigars. He looked around. There she was, an auburn-haired, milky-skinned beauty of the type which Dublin used to export in great numbers. Possibly her father or grandfather had come over on a cattle boat. Now, she looked as if her clothes had come from Paris. Seated on the arm of a chair, she drew at her cigarette and exhaled, and stared coldly at the policeman through the smoke. Ah, well, sometimes they were friendly, sometimes they weren't.

Martineau was wondering if Dixie had ever seen P. C. Ainslie's red-haired dancer. Perhaps he had. Perhaps, even, he had seen her and been rebuffed. Martineau hoped so.

Dixie interrupted his thoughts. "Never mind the wench. What do you want?"

"I'm bringing you information. There was a bogus police raid on the Gee Gee Club tonight. A crowd of ring-tailed baboons from Birmingham or some place. We've got them all inside."

"Why tell me? I don't have any interest in the Gee Gee."

"Thought you'd like to know. Since that raid there's been another one, on the Churlham Drill Hall. Submachine guns and side arms were taken."

Dixie shrugged. "I.R.A."

"Not I.R.A. Have another guess."

"No, it's your turn."

"My guess is that a certain shower of criminal lunatics is in possession of some red-hot money. There's been a move from outside, with the purpose of finding that money and hijacking it. So they've armed themselves. The next lot to interfere is going to get mowed down."

"And serve them right, too," said Dixie heartily. "I'm dead against this mob stuff."

"You might be dead, full stop."

"Not me. At one time I might have been interested, but now, as you know, I'm strictly legit. Have been for years."

"We'll skip that," the policeman said as he turned to go. "I know how legitimate you are. I'm advising you to keep your fingers out of it."

Dixie smiled. "Good night," he said.

"Legit!" Martineau growled as he opened the door of his car. "That character wasn't even born legit."

TWENTY-ONE
THE OTHER SIDE

As BEN OLNEY drove his pickup truck back from the Churlham Drill Hall to the Olney Works, the evening traffic was just right for him. It was not sparse enough to allow his vehicle to be noticed, and yet not heavy enough to delay him unduly. But the convenient mobility of the traffic was no comfort to him. He was worried. Full realization of the error of his association with out-and-out criminals pressed down like a weight on his brain. This latest act of robbery in which he had been forced to join seemed to him to be a prelude to tragedy.

He moved one hand from the wheel and touched the loaded revolver in his pocket. That weapon was symbolic of the condition to which his affairs had deteriorated. If any policeman tried to stop the truck, Ben was supposed to shoot him. Those were his orders, given after a unanimous decision by the three men who were concealed under the canvas sheet in the back of the truck.

He realized that it was Ernie Rapp who had forced him to emerge from a position of comparative security and walk the knife-edge of peril. That little weasel had persuaded him to join in the successful attempt to take Lew Cory and Long Cue Lan-

141

caster from police custody by telling him that he knew a place
where they could hide. After the escape he had coolly announced
that the place he had had in mind was the unused upper floor of
the Chapel of Rest at the Olney Works. He had been quite
logical about it. He had explained that since the announcement
of a reward by the Northern Steel Corporation, no thieves'
kitchen in the city was safe for the fugitives. Ben was the only
man they could trust. They could trust him because he could not
betray them without betraying himself. The other two miscreants
had agreed with him. Upstairs at the Chapel of Rest there was a
toilet, and water. Ben would find them something to eat. They
would keep away from windows and show no lights. They would
be safe until it was time to move from there and get out of the
country.

Ben burned with anger when he remembered how they had
ignored his objections. He had pointed out that he could betray
himself hopelessly by harboring them. He had informed them
that discovery of himself as an accomplice would ultimately lead
to the discovery of the hidden money. "Stop nattering," Long
Cue had told him, and Rapp had said, "Nobody's going to find
out nothin'."

So they had installed themselves, and they had been quiet until
Gerry Gee's phone call had started the present madness. The
club owner's excitement about interference by Dixie Costello had
not communicated itself to Ben. He could not quite see how a
mobster might hunt for fugitives more successfully than the
police. He passed the message on to Cory, expecting that confident scoundrel to laugh about it. But Cory did not laugh. His
comment was a brief obscenity, uttered with immeasurable ma-
lignancy. He told the others, and Ben was appalled by their reception of the news. Rapp gibbered with anxious fury and Long
Cue cursed bitterly.

"He can bring a score of hardnecks against us," Long Cue
said. "We can't fight that crowd with sticks. We need guns."

"Steady," Ben replied. "If you start any shooting around here,
the whole job's ruined. Anyway, how can Costello find you here?"

"You don't know Costello. He's a clever bastard."

"I know where there's some guns," Rapp said. "Churlham
Drill Hall. I did that place not so long ago. I got all the liquor

out of the mess. If there's nobody hangin' about, it'll be a snip."

Against his will Ben was elected driver. He had to use the truck because Rapp—moved by superstition, probably—refused to ride in the brake. He took the three to Churlham, and as Rapp had predicted, it was an easy job. He saw the gloating excitement of Rapp and Lancaster over the possession of sub-machine guns, and he noticed that Cory also seemed to be affected by having the means of wholesale slaughter in his hands. His sense of impending disaster really began to oppress him then. It was obvious that the power to kill and the prospect of doing it intoxicated these men to the extent that they could not think clearly.

Rapp had spent almost the whole of his brief military service in detention and had never been trained in the use of firearms. "Show me how to load it, Lew," he begged, fondly balancing a T.S.M.G. in his hands. "Boy, I'll be sorry for any perisher who tries to stop me."

That hint of an inadequately controlled desire to kill brought Cory to his senses. He said, "I'll show you later. We've got what we came for. Let's get out of here."

Hiding their weapons under their coats, they returned to the truck. They had left it in a deserted thoroughfare between a rail-way embankment and a recreation ground. The three with sub-machine guns lay flat in the back of the truck and Ben covered them with canvas. They started the journey back to the Olney Works, and Ben had time to think.

It was now very clear to him that his opinions no longer had any weight with the others. They had forgotten that he was a man of ideas. They looked upon him as a mere apprentice in crime. Since Costello's name had been mentioned, they had thought only of acquiring the means to oppose the mobster by force. Beyond that they had not seemed to look. Well, today Rapp had been to see his maritime connection and had arranged for Cory and Long Cue to go with him to South Africa. The ship was sailing, Rapp had said evasively, in a day or two. He would not give the name of the vessel, and Ben doubted if he had truthfully named its destination.

So he was saddled with a trigger-happy trio for "a day or two." He was not afraid that Dixie Costello would find them, but he was terribly nervous about Martineau. A murder had been committed at the Olney Works. The place had been searched. Martineau had looked thoughtfully at both Ben and his foreman, Luther Quaint. At any moment he might decide to search again.

There and then Ben became convinced that Martineau would search again, and quite soon. The conviction led him to an inescapable conclusion. If he did not act quickly to save himself, Cory, Rapp and Long Cue would ruin him.

He stopped the truck at the back door of the Chapel of Rest. He alighted, and saw the white blurs of three faces as the canvas was turned back. "Don't move for a minute," he whispered. "I'll look around."

He circled the building and returned. He unlocked the back door and opened it wide. "Turn right, straight down into the cellar," he said. "You can have the light on down there while you see to your guns."

The three accepted the suggestion without question. They scrambled out of the truck and trooped through the doorway. Ben could hear their low-voiced, lighthearted comments as they groped their way down into the cellar. He followed, closing and locking the back door. He also closed the door at the cellar head before he switched on the light.

In the cellar, his three accomplices were blinking, and looking around. "All right," he said. "Make it slippy. I've got to work tomorrow."

Cory began to explain the action of a T.S.M.G. to Rapp, while Long Cue watched with interest. Ben was standing behind Cory, whom he considered to be the danger man. He took his revolver from his pocket, cocked it, and shot Cory in the back of the head at a range of four inches. Cory slumped forward into Long Cue's arms. Over the fallen man's drooping head, Ben put a bullet between Long Cue's startled eyes from a distance of two feet. The two bodies crashed down onto an old sofa. Ben turned in time to stop Rapp's cornered-rat leap with a bullet in the chest. Rapp tottered backward. Ben followed, shooting him twice more, aiming at the heart.

He stood for a moment looking down at his handiwork, rather surprised that none of the three made a further move, scarcely realizing that they would never move again. Lord, he thought, how easy to kill three men. He had killed them as easily as they had killed his father.

He opened the single small box of ammunition which he carried, and reloaded his revolver. He put the weapon in his pocket, and looked at his watch. It was not yet eleven o'clock. He went upstairs, putting out the light. Before he opened the back door he lit a cigarette. He needed it. Standing on the back doorstep he smoked the cigarette, concealing the glow with his cupped hand. Distant traffic noises came to his ears. Once, distant too, there was a bray of raucous adolescent laughter. But in his vicinity there were no sounds, and nothing moved.

He set off, moving silently around the buildings of the Olney Works. There was nobody. He began to feel sure that his shots had not been heard, or at least not heeded.

He was already considering the problem which the three bodies presented. He could not repeat the mortuary trick, his own design which others had so stupidly and unsuccessfully duplicated. He could set a lighted candle among shavings in the cellar, and soak the old furniture with paraffin. The fire would start while he was lying in bed, with the housekeeper somehow made aware of his presence. But before he started a fire he would have to move the Northern Steel money, and that would be inconvenient. Besides, the fire might not totally destroy the bodies. And in any case it seemed a pity to burn down the Chapel of Rest, even though it was insured.

Then the great idea came to Ben. It was so simple that he had to grin. He thought of the muscular effort which it would entail, and felt sure that he could do it. He decided on the place. It was in the countryside beyond Boyton, and Boyton was eight miles away.

The question of equipment was resolved while he was walking back to the workshop. There he picked up hacksaw, glass cutter and case opener. From his office drawer he took an electric torch, and from a dusty, cluttered corner behind the filing cabinet he dragged out a pair of gum boots. The gum boots were big enough to be worn as overboots, and they had been bought for that purpose.

Returning to the Chapel of Rest, Ben put his tools in the cab

145

of the truck. Then he started the most dangerous part of the operation, knowing full well that if the police came upon him now the game was lost, utterly and finally. It was hard work dragging the three bodies up the cellar steps and putting them into the truck, but he did it without pause. When the bodies were covered by the canvas sheet, he returned to the cellar and picked up the T.S.M.G. which Cory had loaded. Though Ben had been sickened by a previous instruction about firearms, he was now prepared to shoot anyone who tried to stop him while he was transporting the three bodies. He put the submachine gun on the seat beside him before he started the truck. He still had the revolver in his pocket.

The journey to Boyton was uneventful. Ben drove carefully, restraining an urge to push on and complete his awful task. It *was* awful. Shocking. He admitted that to himself. But he was quite certain that it would never be a classic murder case, because nobody would ever know what had happened to Cory, Lancaster and Rapp.

The place he sought was one of the smallest of its kind, and he had chosen it for that reason. It was secluded, set well back from the road and hidden among trees. Except for the gate-keeper's lodge at the entrance to the grounds there was no house near it. This was because its chimneys emitted a fallout which nobody liked to breathe. It was called the Hallwood Crematorium.

Because it was a small crematorium, Hallwood had no night staff. The men employed there usually locked the place up at five o'clock in the afternoon and went home for the day. There were no bars on the windows because there was nothing to steal. It was a place avoided by children and lovers. For Ben's purpose it was ideal.

He drove past the locked gates of the grounds, and noted that the lodge was in darkness. At the end of the long, high, front wall he turned a corner and drove slowly, without lights, along a narrow, stony lane which would take him within sixty yards of the crematorium itself. He stopped the truck at the nearest point, and alighted. There the boundary wall was only five feet high. But it was high enough. He looked at it and sighed. It was going to be hard work.

Ben was a stronger man than most, but the task of getting Cory's slack deadweight over the wall was almost too much for him. He never hated the man more than when he strained to raise that solid bulk up to shoulder height. Finally he managed to get his shoulder under the body and rest some of its weight on the top of the wall. He heaved, and turned quickly to thrust with both hands. Cory rolled over the wall and landed with hardly a sound on the soft ground at the other side.

Ben had to rest before he started to handle the almost equally difficult body of Long Cue. After Cory and Long Cue, Rapp seemed to be no weight at all.

When the three bodies were over the wall, Ben put on his gum boots. He put on some old driving gloves which were in the cab of the truck, picked up his housebreaking tools, and climbed over the wall. The trees in that part of the grounds had been planted. They were well spaced, and there were no brambles or other thorny growth. Underfoot was soft leaf mold. Ben did not know whether or not it would show footprints, and as long as he was wearing the gum boots he did not care.

On his first trip to the crematorium he took Rapp's body with him, dragging it by the ankles. He knew that nothing would fall out of the pockets because he had emptied them at the Olney Works. When he reached the crematorium he inspected the back door. It was on the latch. He went to a window and used his diamond near the catch. In a minute the window was open. He climbed over the sill and immediately emerged from the building by the door, leaving it unlatched.

He made two arduous journeys to bring up Cory and Long Cue. When all three bodies were lying just inside the door, he closed it and put on the lights. He was in a room about twenty feet by thirty, with a dirty concrete floor. On one side was a curtained aperture through which laden coffins would glide after mourners had left the occupants to their fate and turned away. On the other side were the two incinerators, invariably called ovens by local undertakers. They did indeed look like ovens.

Broad rollers of shining steel ran from the curtains of the ovens, so that coffins could be moved with a minimum of noise and effort. In a corner of the room there was a huge pestle and mortar, with which charred bones could be pounded to dust.

Ben opened an oven door by raising it by means of a chain over a pulley. He saw that the big coal-gas jets could be ignited by a small pilot jet which was still burning. He dragged up Cory's body and manhandled it on to the rollers. With a long fire rake he pushed it into the oven. He moved the lever which controlled the flow of gas. The foot-long jets of flame came up with a soft roar, their bright points licking through the bars of the grid. "Burn in hell, Cory," he panted fiercely, and lowered the oven door.

Rapp and Long Cue had to share the other oven, and Ben threw in his gum boots after them. Assured that the gas was burning steadily, he turned out the light and departed. In order to avoid leaving his shoe prints anywhere near the prints of the gum boots, he made a detour. He followed a path which led to a locked rear gate. He climbed over the gate and returned to the truck, and slumped wearily into the driver's seat. Though desperately tired, he was not yet done with Cory, Long Cue and Rapp. He intended to return and rake their hot bones out of the ovens, and pound them to unidentifiable ashes, and throw the ashes out of doors for the airs of night to blow away. While he was waiting for the time to do that, he had work to do at the Chapel of Rest. He would have to inspect, to see what traces of murder he had left in the cellar. And evidence of his victims' brief sojourn upstairs would have to be destroyed. And somehow he would have to get rid of that collection of stolen firearms.

He drove back to the Olney Works. Traffic was sparse. But his journey was uninterrupted and, as far as he could tell, unnoticed. When he alighted at the Chapel of Rest he looked at his watch and was surprised to see that the time was barely half an hour after midnight.

He went down into the cellar, and was relieved to find that there was no blood on the floor or the steps. There were two big patches of it on the old sofa. He opened his knife, and cut and ripped until he had removed the dusty plush cover and the padding beneath it. He went across to the garage and returned with a small quantity of paraffin. After soaking the mass of upholstery with paraffin he stuffed it into the rusty old wash boiler in the corner. It leapt into flame at the touch of a match.

He had seen nobody on his journey to and from the garage. It occurred to him that his activities could not go on unseen and uninterrupted forever. It would be better, he thought, for him to get rid of the stolen guns while he had the chance. He could dump them in almost any quiet spot, so long as it was far enough away from his own premises.

He filled his pockets with small boxes of ammunition and stuffed T.S.M.G. magazines inside his shirt. With a little arranging he was able to stuff the four revolvers into his belt. He tucked the two submachine guns under his arm, and then he remembered with a pang of fear that there was a loaded submachine gun still lying on the seat of the truck. If any bobby on night duty should come nosing around and see that gun!

He hurried up the cellar steps and turned out the light. He unlocked the back door and stood in the doorway listening. All was quiet. Nothing moved.

He stepped out of the doorway, moving toward the truck. He looked to left and right. On his right, at the corner of the building, he saw a dark figure and the unmistakable outline of a policeman's helmet. He knew why the policeman was standing quietly there. He had seen the truck and had heard the back door being opened. After the manner of his kind, he had waited to see who would emerge.

There was one aspect of the situation which Ben had not immediately perceived. The P.C. not only wanted to see who was emerging from a darkened building at night, he also wanted to see what that person was carrying. Ben reached the truck, but he was still holding the Tommy guns when the policeman brought his flashlight into play. The torch was a powerful one. Ben was bathed in light, festooned with firearms like a comic-opera brigand.

He did not pause in his movements, but put the useless, unloaded Tommy guns in the back of the truck. The policeman did not move, or speak. Ben could not remember which one of the revolvers in his belt was the loaded one. With his mind in a turmoil but with an air of calmness, he reached into the cab of the truck and brought out the loaded T.S.M.G. The light went out and the policeman vanished round the corner. Ben heard the quick patter of his retreating footsteps, and knew from the way he ran that he was young and fit. Young he may have been, but he was not green. At any rate not green enough to stay, unarmed, and get into an argument with a man who held a sub-machine gun. Ben realized that of course he would have been informed of the Drill Hall robbery. And now he would know at least one of the robbers.

Ben ran to the corner. He was in time to see the P.C. leap onto the top of the perimeter wall and drop down out of sight. Ben ran to the wall and leaned over it. He saw the P.C. running, bent double, on the other side. He raised the submachine gun, but did not open fire. Was anything to be gained by killing the running man? He could not think clearly about that. The whole incident had been too unexpected.

He saw the policeman break cover and cross the street. He turned a corner, and the sound of his running feet began to die away. He would be making for the nearest telephone. Very well. There was yet time for Ben to save the situation.

Now he knew what to do. The necessity for quick flight at any time was one of the things he had prepared for. He had even considered what he would do if he had to escape from the city at night. Another of his undertaker's ideas, this one; a crazy idea but quite practical. He ran back to the truck and dumped all his armament except the loaded revolver. Entering the Chapel of Rest, he switched on the ground-floor lights. He went into a room where a coffin lay on a bier. Taking one end of the coffin he gently lowered it to the ground, so that the coffin itself was propped almost upright against the bier. He went into another room and returned with an empty coffin, which he laid on the bier. From the upright coffin he pulled out the body—a tall but emaciated old woman—and caught it as it fell. He lifted the shrouded figure carefully, and laid it decently in the new coffin. He deftly straightened the shroud, and turned to the upright coffin, examining it briefly to make sure that it was the one he wanted. He picked it up and carried it outside, and put it on the truck. The coffin had no lid; he did not need a lid.

He turned out the lights and locked up the Chapel of Rest, for he was beginning to see, now, that he had a better chance of avoiding the law's penalties if he left things in order. He drove the truck round to the workshop, knowing exactly what he wanted from there. He had it ready in the office: a few screws in a twist of paper, a screwdriver, two small clamps, and a six-foot length of white pine one inch by three. He put this equipment into the truck and drove away. Cautiously returning after making his phone call, the young P.C. saw him go. The P.C. wondered if that was the outline of a coffin he could see on the truck. He thought that it might be. He was the first member of the Granchester City Police to realize that the Northern Steel plunder could have been hidden in the bottom of a coffin, under a body. He ran to the telephone again.

As he drove away from the Olney Works, Ben fully understood that he was a fugitive, but he hoped that this plight was only temporary. He was thankful now that he had not fired even a single shot at the policeman. Such an act could not have been explained away. As it was, the explanation could be that the young and probably inexperienced P.C. *thought* that he had seen Ben with an armful of submachine guns. He had seen him only for a second or two, at night. Ben could dream up a feasible story and produce two or three long clamps, or something of the kind, and say, "These were what the constable saw." Or maybe he could deny that he had been there at all. If the P.C. did not happen to know him, he might even be unable to identify him.

He thought there was a chance that all might yet be well, provided he could escape and put the Northern Steel money in the second hiding place which he had had in mind. Of course the police would suspect him now, but they would not be able to prove anything. All the same, it was a great pity that the young P.C. had appeared at the Olney Works. Now Ben would not have time to return to the crematorium and complete the obliteration of Cory, Rapp and Long Cue. The past identities of three crumbling skeletons, one large, one small, and one very tall, would be no mystery to the police. But even if they could prove identity they would have no evidence to associate Ben with those three. They had never seen him in such company.

He knew that he must have got blood on his clothes when he was handling those three bodies. Well, he had a change of clothes at the place he was making for. If only he could get there! The police would already be setting up their damned cordon. They would be looking everywhere for him.

He thought that he could elude them. He had had time to plan a way of doing that.

He sighed. If only it was over. The worry of it all was enough to drive a man mad.

TWENTY-TWO

IT WAS ten minutes to one when Martineau was informed that a heavily armed man had been seen leaving the Olney Chapel of Rest. The issue of Webley-Scott automatic pistols to some of his own men had already been authorized, and he immediately sent off two carloads of armed detectives, one team going to Ben Olney's house and the other to his foreman's.

He assumed that the pickup truck had been used recently, or was about to be used, and he caused a local Express Message to be circulated, asking for news of the truck and giving the instruction that the driver must be arrested. This order stressed the probability that the driver was armed with a submachine gun, and it insisted that unnecessary risks must not be taken.

At five minutes past one Martineau received the second piece of information concerning the Olney Works. He did not doubt the none-too-positive statement that the truck had been carrying a coffin when it was driven away. He made the correct surmise. Who had been hiding stolen money in a coffin, under a body? Ben Olney or his foreman? From the description of the P.C. who had seen the armed man, it looked as if it might be Ben.

Martineau at once set into motion the well-tried and usually successful scheme for blocking the ways out of the city. Ten

153

minutes later he was informed that Luther Quaint the foreman had been in bed when the police called at his house. "Borrow his keys for the Olney Works," he said. "If he won't lend them, put him under arrest on suspicion and take him there with his keys. Wait for me there and don't stick your neck out."

Five minutes later he learned that Ben Olney was missing from home, and at once many things seemed to fall into place. It was probable that Ben had been the Northern Steel gang's treasurer, that he had hidden the stolen money for them, and that his father had somehow discovered it, probably because it had been hidden in a coffin of unusual dimensions. Because he had discovered something his death had been arranged. Ben had not been the first man in history to have a hand in the murder of his own father. It was somewhat incredible, but the evidence seemed to indicate it. What on earth was Ben Olney doing, playing around with men like Long Cue Lancaster and Ernie Rapp? That certainly was incredible.

Martineau put out a further Express Message, to All Districts, to the effect that Ben Olney was wanted for robbery with violence, and for interview in connection with the murder of Webster Olney, with a footnote stating that he was armed.

The chief inspector's next move was to the Olney Works. A brief, cautious personal search assured him that the place was deserted. He called up his men, and directed a more thorough search. The condition of the sofa in the cellar was noted, and the remains of burnt fabric were found in the wash boiler. A stain which Ben had overlooked was found at the bottom of the untouched upholstery of the back of the sofa. To Martineau it looked like blood. He cut out the piece of material for dispatch to the laboratory, but it gave him no real clue to what had happened in the cellar. It never entered his head that one amateur criminal could dispose of Cory, Lancaster and Rapp.

Upstairs in the Chapel of Rest the signs of occupancy which Ben, with knowledge, had intended to sweep away were not noticed by the police. None of them had the slightest suspicion that the three fugitives had been hiding there. This lack of insight was mainly due to a preconception on their part. From the beginning they had all believed that Rapp and his friends were being sheltered by some woman.

From what he had seen and heard, Martineau was inclined to believe that Ben had now gone to join the others, taking the stolen money and the Drill Hall armament with him. Had he robbed the armory without assistance? It looked as if he might have done. From this latest phase of the investigation he was emerging as a very black sheep indeed.

From the Olney Works Martineau went to the Olney house at Highfield. Mrs. Harrison, the housekeeper, having loudly complained that her first sound sleep since Sunday had been ruined by the police, was still sitting in the kitchen comforting herself with cups of tea. She glowered at Martineau. He did not mind. He proceeded to question her at once, because he believed that her grumpiness concealed intense curiosity. She would answer questions in the hope of learning something.

"I don't think Ben will be coming home tonight," he told her. "He's gone off somewhere and I'd like to get in touch with him."

"He'll come home," she said. "I've never known him go off in the middle of the week."

"Does that mean he sometimes goes off at weekends?"

"Every weekend, except for last Saturday when his poor father was murdered. Ben's gone off Saturday night an' come home Sunday every week for a twelve month or more."

Martineau was surprised. That was something he should have known. He had not known it because he had not asked. There had been no reason to ask.

"Where does he go?"

"If you can find that out, you're more clever nor I am. Stayin' wi' friends, he always said."

"Did he take pajamas with him, or anything like that?"

"No. He never took nothin', as far as I could see. Happen he had some pajamas at the place where he stayed."

"Well, I suppose you were a bit curious. It's only natural. Didn't you ever find any sort of clue as to where he went or the sort of people he met?"

"No. I looked often enough, but I never found nothin'."

"Did you ever find traces of lipstick on his shirt collar, or anything like that?"

"Nothin'. An' that's the truth. Like you said, I were wonderin'. But he's a close 'un, is Ben. Tell 'em nothin', that's his motto."

Martineau asked more questions, but got no further. He examined Ben's personal things in search of a clue, and did not find one. He asked one more question, and then he went away. The question concerned Ben's car. The answer was the one he had hoped for. On Saturday nights Ben had always gone away in his car, and returned in it on Sundays.

On his way back to Headquarters the chief inspector thought about Ben, and came to the conclusion that he was a worthy opponent for any policeman. He was a man who prepared. The brilliant idea for the changing of bodies at the mortuary must have been his. This led to the inference that he had not planned the murder of his father, because he would not have allowed the clumsy second attempt at substitution. He had merely condoned his father's murder.

Ben's apparent candor had been deceptive. He had told the truth up to a point. And he had had confidence in his ability to deceive. The use of his own firm's truck in various escapades had been a blatant double bluff, made in the expectation that the police would not believe that a guilty man could be foolhardy enough to draw attention to himself in that way.

And now Ben was on the run. Martineau wondered, now, whether he was going to join his accomplices or whether he was trying to reach his weekend retreat. Was the flight an attempt to escape permanently with £29,000, assuming that Ben really had it, or would Ben find another hiding place for it and then return with empty hands and the best story he could invent? No doubt he would be weighing the evidence against himself at that very moment, intending to plot his future course of action on the assessment.

After the raid on the Gee Gee Club, P. C. Ainslie found that he was, temporarily, a forgotten man. He made out his report, and transcribed the statement he had taken from Jud Wragg. After that he had nothing to do but wait about. All his superiors were too busy to find him a job. The time was a little after ten o'clock. He could go quietly home, but that seemed a tame way to end the day. There was one thing he could do. He was supposed to be looking after Cleo Patton. He could go round to her flat and make sure that she was still unharmed.

On the way to the flat he called at a shop where hot pies and peas, chips, black puddings, tripe, and other supper dishes were sold. He arrived at the flat bearing a parcel of chips and two hot steak puddings in little basins. Cleo seemed to be pleased but, she said, she had had some supper. Joe replied that it was not the first time he had eaten two steak puddings, and it would not be the last.

After the supper had been eaten, they played records for a while. Cleo remarked, not too sternly, that it was getting late. Joe agreed with her, and stayed where he was. He brought up the subject of marriage, and then they made love. They made love playfully, and they made love passionately. Joe adored her.

It was half past one in the morning when Cleo decided that she needed some fresh air. "I'll never sleep tonight," she complained.

Joe was not quite happy about that. The streets would be deserted, except perhaps for enemies. A recent night adventure was still vivid in his mind. With men like Cory and Lancaster, one could never take chances. "You're safer indoors," he said. "Besides, I have my orders."

"I don't take orders from Mr. Martineau," Cleo told him. "And I'm not under arrest either."

He had already noted that she was occasionally willful, sometimes perverse, and quite often ready to show that she had a temper. Well, she was a woman, and a spirited one.

"Be patient," he said. "The job will soon be cleared."

"I've been patient all evening. Nobody will see us in the dark. Just a little walk, and then I'll make you a nice cup of coffee."

He had also noticed that she could wheedle. He said, "Somebody might see us as soon as we step out of the front door."

"We'll go out the back way. They won't even know about that. Nobody ever uses it. We won't be out long."

"All right," he said. "Just a little stroll."

So, about the time when Martineau was questioning Ben Olney's housekeeper, Joe and Cleo were strolling and enjoying the cool night air. Once more Joe was talking about marriage.

"They're building a dozen new police houses at Honey Green," he said. "They're going to be smashers. A nice big garden, and that."

"I'd love a garden," Cleo said dreamily. "I've never lived where there was a garden."

"Well, if you'll promise to marry me, I can apply for one. There will be a lot of fellows after 'em, but I'll have as good a chance as the next man."

"But what about my business?"

"We can talk about the business any time. If we want one of those houses I'll have to get my name down."

"Suppose you don't get one?"

"I have a few hundred saved. If I can't get a police house I'll buy one through a building society. I'll guarantee you a nice house and a nice garden."

"He woos me with the aid of the building society," she mocked.

"Oh, hell, Cleo. I'm in love with you."

"I'll marry you, darling, with or without the building society."

"Bless you." He seized her and kissed her. They leaned against a six-foot steel parapet. "You've made me the happiest man in the world," he whispered. "And I'll make you the happiest woman."

She kissed him. "You already have."

The sound of splashing came to his ears. He looked at the painted steel against which he leaned and realized that he was standing on a bridge over the Fosse Canal. It was not the bridge under which Martineau had found dead men's clothing, but one farther out from the center of the city.

He listened. The splashing continued. It was not loud, but it could have been made by someone in the water, struggling to keep afloat.

"Just a minute," he said. He disengaged himself from the arms of his love, and reached to pull himself up an inch or two and look over the parapet. He was in time to see the flash of a paddle some distance away. The man, and the craft he was propelling, faded away into the darkness.

"That's unusual," he said as he turned away from the parapet. "Some fellow is paddling a canoe in the dark."

He was going to take her in his arms again. She put both hands on his chest and held him away with all her strength.

"No more," she said dryly. "Go and have a swim."

"Nay, love," he protested. "I had to look. It might've been somebody drowning."

She realized that he was right. She was too touchy. If she was going to marry a policeman, she might as well be married to a good one.

She took his arm, and hugged it, and turned him toward home. "I'm sorry, darling," she said. "Come on. Coffee."

TWENTY-THREE

BEFORE Martineau left his desk that night he put out a full description of Ben Olney's car, in the hope that some police officer had noticed it at one regular place on a number of Saturday nights and Sunday mornings. He also alerted the county police on this matter. It was hoped that Ben and his loot were still penned in the city, but nothing could be taken for granted with a man as resourceful as he had shown himself to be.

After that there was nothing else to do. Everything was being done to find Ben and the other fugitives, or to catch them if they made a move. The docks, the railway stations, the bus stations, the airport and the roads were picketed. The number of the pickup truck was known to every constable, and in fact every vehicle which moved in the city later that night was stopped by the police. All known haunts of criminals were raided and searched. All known or suspected gambling houses were raided too, because it was believed possible that Ben might be in his present predicament because he was a secret gambler. The Gee Gee Club was searched yet again, on the off-chance that he might have taken refuge there.

At four o'clock in the morning there was no news. Martineau went home and had three hours' sleep. He never slept at the office. He preferred to sleep in his own bed even if it were for only one hour.

He was back in his office by nine o'clock. He found that P. C. Ainslie was waiting to see him.

"Yes?" Martineau asked. He looked tired and he sounded tired, but he was not grumpy.

"It's an idea I've got, sir."

"About what?"

"About Olney. You might think I'm a fool."

"I'll listen, and whatever I think, I won't say it."

"Well, sir. About two o'clock this morning I saw a man paddling something which could have been a canoe, along the Fosse Canal."

"And you think it might have been Olney?"

"I didn't think anything till this morning when I heard about the coffin. A coffin is supposed to be watertight, isn't it?"

"A coffin? You think he could have navigated a *coffin* along the canal? Wouldn't it turn over?"

"Not if he fixed up something in the nature of an outrigger."

Martineau grinned. "It's an ingenious idea. Which way was he going?"

"North, sir. I saw him from the York Road bridge."

"Mmmm. A coffin would be a bit low in the water with a man in it, but I suppose it would float all right with something to balance it. The canal would be calm, with no current. And any bit of wood would do for a paddle. It's feasible. I think we'll make a few inquiries while we're waiting for somebody to find the truck."

Ainslie departed. Martineau looked up the telephone number of the local office of Inland Waterways. He made the call, and was put in touch with the man in charge.

"No," he was told. "At the moment we have no private craft of any kind on the Fosse Canal. Not in this locality, at any rate. No permission to use the canal has been given either. I'll phone around, and find out if a lockkeeper has seen any trespassers."

After that he sent an inquiry round the divisions, asking for details of any incident which had been reported on or near the Fosse Canal during the past sixteen hours.

Then he had to go into court and attend the appearance of

his newest batch of prisoners, and hear Clay apply for a remand in custody.

When he came out of court the news from Boyton hit him like a blow in the face. Because it involved three unofficial cremations he made an accurate guess at the start. When he heard a descripion of the charred bodies—long, large, short—he was certain. He was dourly tolerant of the excitement which came along the wire from Boyton. The chief of detectives there thought that he had a triple murder on his hands. Martineau knew where those murders had been committed: in his own manor, Granchester.

It transpired that there had been some delay before the Boyton police were informed. The first man on duty at the crematorium had arrived at eight o'clock and had noticed that the ovens were going at full blast. Assuming that there had been some negligence on the part of one of his mates, he turned down the gas. A few minutes later the foreman arrived. Because he did not want to get any of his mates into trouble, the first workman made no mention of what he had done. But the foreman noticed that the ovens were very hot, and the truth came out. The foreman opened the ovens, and saw the remains inside. He had sufficient discretion to leave them untouched, even with a fire rake.

The direction of crematorium affairs was in the hands of the manager of the town's Public Cleansing Department. That official was informed by telephone, at his home. He had his breakfast and went to his office to attend to one or two important matters before he drove to the crematorium to see what all this nonsense was about. When he saw he was appalled. He called the police.

After that there was some quick and efficient preliminary work. The hot bones were carefully lifted out of the rapidly cooling ovens. Their dimensions were roughly measured. Two punctured and riven skulls and one shattered sternum were noted. It was assumed that this damage had been done by bullets, and that these were now shapeless little cakes of metal which would be found among the ashes.

That information was enough for Martineau. He did not think that there was anything to be gained by going to Boyton.

He had lost three prisoners, and it was no use crying over them. He still had to find the man who had cremated them.

He went back to work, and learned that the much-sought pickup truck had been found in a thoroughfare called Back Nicholl Street. This fact gave no support to the floating coffin theory. The street was at least a quarter of a mile away from the Fosse Canal. The truck contained neither a coffin nor a collection of firearms. It was not likely that a hunted man would carry those things a quarter of a mile through lighted streets. Martineau did not know the weight of the average coffin, but he assumed that it would be fairly heavy.

More light on the matter came through a reply to Martineau's canal inquiry. There had been a report of trivial damage to the gate of Mulligan's scrap-metal yard, on Canal Road. Someone had forced the hasp which held the padlock but there had been no attempt to enter Mulligan's office. There had been no further damage and apparently nothing at all had been stolen.

Martineau told Devery to bring his car round. The two of them drove to Mulligan's, and found it between Canal Road and the canal itself. Though the canal was not used for the transport of scrap, there was a little wharf.

Mulligan, a large man in both height and girth, looked somewhat shamefaced when he saw who it was stepping out of the C.I.D. car. "Mr. Martineau," he said. "I'm surprised to see you. It was only a little bit of damage. I was in two minds about mentioning it."

"I'm glad you did, Mr. Mulligan," said the policeman. He stared around, while Devery went back to look at the damaged gate.

Like any other scrapyard, the place was an eyesore. He walked round among rusty, broken car bodies, piles of worn-out components, a pile of old tram lines, heaps of assorted metal debris, heaps of old oil drums. He stopped when he came to an orderly pile of two-gallon petrol cans.

Some of the cans were complete with screw-on caps, others were without. "Mr. Mulligan," he called, "do you know how many cans there should be here?"

"I don't," said Mulligan. "But I can find out."

He went into his office. Two minutes later he came out and said, "Four hundred and eighty, unless one or two have been pinched."

Martineau counted. The pile was ten by ten, five tiers high. The fifth tier was incomplete. He climbed onto the pile of tram lines, so that he could look down and count. There were seventy-eight cans in the fifth tier.

"Two missing," he said.

"Somebody must have helped themselves to a couple," said Mulligan. "It isn't worth bothering about."

Martineau nodded absently. He was beginning to believe in the canal theory. "Do you know Ben Olney?" he asked.

"Sure, I knew his dad, too. I sometimes have odd and ends of timber, going cheap. I sometimes get quite good stuff."

"Has Ben been to see you since you acquired these petrol cans?"

"Aye. Two or three times, I should think. What's he got to do with petrol cans?"

Martineau shook his head, thinking about Ben. He had known about the petrol cans, and no doubt he had had cord in his pocket. He had opened the gate, driven into the yard, and unloaded the coffin. He had tied two petrol cans, complete with cap, to two handles of the coffin: one to port and one to starboard; then he had left the coffin and driven the truck to Back Nicholl Street. He had left it there and walked back to the yard. Somehow he had managed to launch the coffin and get into it. With an empty two-gallon can firmly tied at each side it would not easily capsize. He had paddled steadily away to the north, through the police cordons, out of the city and into the country. It was possible. It was even probable.

Again Martineau shook his head, thinking about Ben. He was awfully glad that he had no professional thieves of that caliber on his manor. The man was much too resourceful. Even when he had been surprised into unplanned action, taking flight with a coffin as baggage, he had put the cumbersome thing to use. Indeed, he had made it be of vital help. And now, after all that, he had a place to go, and a helpmate about whom he had had the foresight to be reticent.

While every other possible inquiry was being made, Martineau decided to give his own attention to the canal theory. When he was back in his office he got out a large-scale map which covered Granchester and an area twenty miles to the north, northeast and northwest. With his finger he followed the course of the Fosse Canal. He estimated that the maximum average speed at which a man could propel a coffin with a makeshift paddle would be two and a half miles an hour, and the farther he went the slower he would go. From this he calculated that the longest distance Ben could have traveled by, say, five o'clock in the morning would be between seven and eight miles. Three miles of that was in the county area.

He went to the county police office in the city and knocked on the door of his old friend Vanbrugh, the county superintendent.

"Come in," Vanbrugh said with a pretense of brusqueness. "I expect you're in trouble again. Always coming to me for help."

"I've got to," the city man retorted. "When we get the goods on our clients they run into your manor, where they know they're safe."

"I'm still hoping we'll get something for you on that Ford Consul."

"I think you might," Martineau agreed. The modern policeman has a phenomenal memory for cars, usually being interested in them and having or hoping to have a car of his own. It was not unlikely that some constable stationed in a village or a small town would know Ben's car quite well and would be able to point out the house which he visited at weekends.

"We still need the gen on the car," he said, as he started to spread his map on the desk, "but this is something else entirely."

He explained the canal theory to Vanbrugh, who was at first entirely skeptical and later only doubtful. He mentioned his calculations. Tracing the course of the canal on the map, he put his finger on the small town of Wrigley, eight miles away. It was a place typical of the region, a little industrial and shopping center in the middle of an area which was neither town nor country. There were dairy farms with rich green fields, but always there was a mill chimney in sight. The farmers and their sons sold eggs and milk to the dairies of Granchester and the farmers' daughters worked in factories nearby.

"Somewhere around there, I'd say," Martineau pronounced. "And not far from the canal."

"I was stationed in Wrigley at one time," said Vanbrugh. "I know it well."

"Can my men work with yours in Wrigley?"

"Why not? They'll be able to show your lot how a good force goes to work."

"When I was looking through Ben's things I snaffled a photo. It looks like a holiday snap taken some years ago, but it's a good enough likeness. I'm having copies made, for showing to people in the usual way. If he's been spending weekends around there for a year or more, somebody ought to recognize him. I'm thinking his girl friend out there might be a widow or a woman parted from her husband. She'll have a home of her own where Ben can stay on his visits."

"I'll put as many men as I can spare into Wrigley. How will you take yours? In a coach?"

"In cars, I think. A coach or a van would be too noticeable. Dixie Costello is trying to put in his thumb. If he gets an inkling that we're making inquiries around Wrigley he might get at Ben before we do."

"Is his intelligence so good?"

"It is indeed. I don't want him around. It would be nice to catch him making the grab, but he's so quick off the mark I daren't risk letting him get near."

With that Martineau folded his map and returned to his own office. The reproduced photographs were ready. Within minutes he sent off his first car to Wrigley. The others followed soon after. Three carloads were enough, he thought, with himself, Devery, Cassidy and Hearn making a fourth.

In Wrigley, Vanbrugh was already on the ground. He first equipped certain of his men with photographs and sent them into the countryside. The small county police station was prominent in the center of the town, and the comings and goings of so many large men in plain clothes attracted attention. Curious townsfolk gathered, and soon the local representative of the Granchester *Evening Guardian* arrived. Martineau and Vanbrugh together asked him, civilly, to be a good boy and wait for his news. He would not promise to wait, but went off to get in contact with his head office. By doing so he missed a good story.

The beginning of the story came from Devery. He had gone off with a county sergeant to set up road blocks, to stop Ben Olney from bolting out of the town when he became aware of what was happening. He came running back before the two officers in charge had finished sending out their teams of leg men.

"A plain van just came into town from Granchester way," he announced. "It came in without being stopped. I happened to be watching it as it went by and I saw someone looking out of the little window at the back. It was the face that stopped a thousand clocks. The Dog."

Martineau was perturbed. The man called Wolfe, nicknamed the Dog, was the biggest, ugliest, and most stupid of Dixie Costello's entourage.

"What was the number?" he asked.

"7454 ZZA. A fairly old green Bedford."

"Can it get out in any other direction?"

"Not now, sir. Not without being pulled up."

Vanbrugh, who was listening, was told that Dixie Costello and his merry men were in the town. He immediately sent out plainclothes men on motorcycles, scooters and bicycles to try to locate the van. "They know every inch of this little spot," he assured Martineau. "They'll soon find it."

Martineau was biting his thumbnail, and that was not a habit of his.

Vanbrugh's prediction was accurate. The van was seen cruising along a little lane on the northern side of the town. The lane was a dead end. The van went back to the main road and then turned along another byway.

"The driver is trying to get out to the north without going through a check point," Vanbrugh said. "He's after something up there."

"Will he manage it?"

"He might, with a bit of luck or a good sense of direction," the county man said. He opened the map of the district. "Here he is, see. Lily Lane. If he finds his way through, he's bound to come out—here."

"In that case, we'd better be waiting for him," said Martineau. "See, the canal follows the road due northeast there. It looks as if Dixie has picked up a bit of vital information somewhere."

TWENTY-FOUR

EIGHT men in two cars traveled northward from Wrigley for a distance of two miles. Vanbrugh with three of his men was in the first car, and Martineau with Devery, Cassidy and Hearn was in the second. Vanbrugh stopped when he was fifty yards short of the side road from which he expected the green van to emerge. He turned off the road and went bumping over rough ground toward a clump of hawthorn bushes. Martineau followed. When both cars were hidden from the side road, the two leaders alighted and stood watching the junction of road and byway through a screen of leaves and twigs.

By the roadside a hundred yards beyond the junction there was a small farm, and opposite the farm there was an inn. The canal ran quite close to the road at that place, and the inn was between the road and the canal. The inn door was open. Martineau looked at his watch and was surprised to see that the time was a little after one o'clock. The inn was legally open for the refreshment of customers.

Because he was not looking directly at the front of the inn, he could not make out its name. But he could see the sign clearly enough. It was a white swan. "Nice little pub," he commented.

"Any drunk who walks out of the back door instead of the front is liable to get cooled off in the canal."

"It used to be a good little business in my day around here," Vanbrugh replied. "I don't know who keeps it now." He turned his head and called quietly, "Fuller!"

A local sergeant got out of the county car and approached. "Who keeps the Swan these days?" Vanbrugh asked.

"A Mrs. Williamson, Eileen Williamson," the sergeant replied. "She's a widow. The licensing bench and the brewery let her carry on with the pub after her husband died. She's straight enough, though I've heard she has a young man who visits her regular." Then he said, "Jesus wept! Why didn't I think of that before?"

"You and your entire section should have thought of it," said Vanbrugh coldly. "That's the sort of local information I've been asking for."

The sergeant was crestfallen. He had let down the county in front of the city, and in the hearing of a C.I.D. superintendent. "I'm sorry, sir," he said.

Martineau saved the day for the sergeant. "Here they come," he said.

The top of the green van could be seen as it rolled along the walled lane. It cautiously entered the main road and turned north. It stopped at the White Swan. The driver came round and opened its rear door. Men emerged. All but the driver went into the inn.

"One, two, three, four, five, six. And the driver," Martineau counted. "Let's go get 'em. We can enter licensed premises without a warrant."

"I'll take the front, you take the back," said Vanbrugh. They ran to their cars.

They backed the cars onto the road and drove to the inn. Vanbrugh stopped close behind the van, and Martineau turned to stop across its front. "Get that driver," he snapped over his shoulder.

The van driver was in his seat. For a moment he stared in dismay, then he put his thumb to the horn. Hearn reached in through the open window and removed the thumb. Then rather unnecessarily he showed the driver the pistol which he still carried. "Make another sound and I'll blow your head off," he growled.

"Stay with him," said Martineau. With Devery and Cassidy he ran round to the back of the inn. Vanbrugh and his men were already at the front door.

Vanbrugh entered to find Dixie Costello and his five men leaning on the bar, and the five were trying to follow their leader's example of looking innocently surprised. Afterward, what had happened was accurately deduced. Dixie had lined his men up at the bar and ordered drinks while he briefly studied the layout of the place. The van driver's blare of warning had made him look out the window and see the arrival of his old enemy, Martineau. "Shed your armament and stand pat," he had ordered, and razors, coshes, and two hand guns had been quickly rubbed clean of fingerprints and thrown under the bench which ran along two sides of the room.

Vanbrugh saw that a white-faced, shaking woman was actually drawing drinks. Costello noted the glance, and smiled. When he smiled all his men smiled. When Martineau arrived, the smile widened.

"Well! Delighted to meet you, my dear fellow! What will you have to drink?"

Martineau understood the situation at once. There would be no charge against Dixie and his mob, except possibly in the matter of carrying offensive weapons.

"Give these men a rubdown," he said to Devery. "See what implements they've got."

He turned to Vanbrugh. "We'd better have two men outside, back and front," he said. "Then you and I will look for Olney."

There was no time for Vanbrugh to answer. When Martineau had finished speaking, the next speaker was a revolver of heavy caliber, somewhere out in front of the inn.

In front of the inn, Hearn had invited the van driver to alight. The man did so. Hearn searched him for weapons, and found none.

"Lucky for you," he said with a grin, and put his own gun in

170

his pocket. He was standing with his back to the inn, and the driver was facing it. Some change—a sudden guardedness—in the driver's expression made him turn. He saw Ben Olney jump down eight feet from the lean-to cart shed of the inn and land lightly on his toes. An open bedroom window above the roof of the shed appeared to have been his means of getting out of the inn.

Ben picked up a leather traveling bag which he must have dropped before he jumped. He began to walk briskly toward Hearn and the van driver, who were no more than sixteen or seventeen yards away. His right hand was in the side pocket of his coat, and the pocket bulged ominously.

Seeing that, Hearn started to bring out his own gun, not as yet with the intention of shooting, but to show that he was armed and could not be shot down with impunity.

Then the driver lost his head. For some reason which was never discovered he elected to take sides against the police. He grabbed Hearn's gun arm with both hands.

Hearn reacted at once. He was a powerful young man, possibly even stronger than Martineau or Cassidy. He was in no position to strike with his fist, so he sidestepped and pulled the man after him as he tried to free his arm. And precisely at that moment Ben brought up his revolver and fired.

The bullet hit the driver, knocking him sideways. The man made a noise like a very sharp intake of breath. He went down on his knees, still clinging to Hearn's arm. Hearn was still moving, frantically trying to free his arm. Ben fired again, and missed. Hearn tore himself free as the driver collapsed. He fired quickly as Ben squeezed the trigger for the third time. He was the better marksman. Ben turned as he fell sprawling. Hearn bounded forward and put his foot on the hand which held the revolver.

Men poured out of the inn. The affray was over.

The van driver seemed to be dead, with a bullet in or near his heart. Hearn was unhurt. Ben had been shot high on the right side, and it was afterward found that his shoulder blade was shattered. He was Vanbrugh's prisoner, having committed murder on Vanbrugh's territory. The county superintendent did not wait for an ambulance. He put both Ben and the van driver into his car and rushed them to the Wrigley Cottage Hospital a mile away. He left the traveling bag in Martineau's care.

The Costello mob had rushed out of the inn with the police. The woman from behind the bar was there also, standing hand to mouth, stricken. Costello himself was staring thoughtfully at the leather bag.

"Yes, Dixie," Martineau said with a satisfied nod. "I think this bag will be holding the stuff you were seeking. Just in case you're mad enough to try to take it . . ." He showed that he had a pistol. "Over your dead body."

"What on earth is he talking about?" Dixie asked of nobody in particular. "All these cowboy capers! It's uncivilized."

Cars were stopping and motorists were watching and listening. Martineau herded everybody back into the inn, and then he closed the doors. "Now then, sergeant," he said. "Continue your search of these men."

Devery obeyed. When he had frisked three of the mobsters and found no weapons, Cassidy muttered something under his breath and started to look beneath the benches. He fished out weapons, holding them daintily to preserve fingerprints. The weapons made a grim collection on the bar.

"Coo, firearms!" said Dixie in a shocked voice. He turned to the woman, who had resumed her place behind the bar. He addressed her sternly. "Madam, you've had Teddy Boys in here. Very bad little Teds, too."

"Shut up!" Martineau snapped. But the damage had been done. The woman had been told what to do.

"I—I don't know how those things got there," she said.

Costello nodded indulgently to her. Now, for her own future safety, she was on his side. He shrugged and held out his open hands to Martineau.

The policeman was not angry. He had taken a quick look at the contents of the bag, and seen a large amount of paper money. The Northern Steel-Verney Barton-Olney job was practically cleared, and the property recovered. Dixie and his men had escaped a minor charge because an investigating officer cannot do everything at once. His slight annoyance about that was neutralized by a reluctant admiration for the man who stood before him. Costello's timing was nearly always perfect. He was deliberate when deliberation was necessary, and like lightning when there was need to be quick.

Martineau asked curiously, "What's your patter about being here when this happened?"

"The sheerest accident, inspector. I thought I'd buy the boys a drink."

"Can you explain how six of you came to be cooped in a van?"

"I'm thinking of buying a farm up here. I wanted to study the lie of the land without being seen."

"The lie of the land! The lie of the century. Why did you turn off to avoid the check point?"

"What check point? The driver was looking for the farm, and he got lost. And now the poor fellow has been shot. Somebody is going to be sorry about that."

"Yes, but not you. I'm taking you all in on reasonable suspicion of carrying offensive weapons, and you'll be held until that trash on the bar has been dusted for prints."

Dixie remained cool. "But, inspector, you're off your manor."

"I'm taking you in," the county sergeant said quickly.

The top mobster did not remove his gaze from Martineau. He spoke in mild sorrow, a tone which made his men grin. "You're only doing this to inconvenience me. You'll have to let me go, you know. And then I'll have to see my lawyer, and seek redress."

"Nobody's going to be sorry about that," said Martineau. "I'm only sorry I moved a bit too quickly. I should have caught you with your hands full of what isn't yours."

"That'll be the day. You'll have a beard that long."

Martineau let it go. He had thwarted Dixie, and that was something. One day he would get him on a serious charge, and get him right. He could afford to wait.

TWENTY-FIVE

FOUR DAYS passed before Martineau was able to talk to Ben Olney. He found him in a private ward at the cottage hospital, with a police guard. Ben was still lying on his back, with his head slightly raised. Martineau had expected him to look pale and ill, but still the change from the ruddy Ben he had known was something of a shock.

"How are you, Ben?" he asked genially.

A certain apprehension vanished from the sick man's face. "I thought you'd be giving me a choking off," he said, and considering the circumstances his voice was quite strong.

"Not me. I'm here to get your story, if you want to give it. I'm supposed to tell you that you're not obliged to, and that anything you say will be taken down in writing and may be given in evidence."

Ben's eyes moved to take in the male clerk whom Martineau had brought along. He was already seated, his open notebook on his knee.

"I might as well," he said. "I know I haven't a cat-in-hell chance of dodging the chop. The firm's lawyer came to see me, and I asked him how I stood. He told me if you shoot at one man and kill another its capital murder just the same. No chance of getting away with manslaughter. Not this time, at any rate."

"You were doing very well until they gave you a gun. You were right smart."

Ben nodded solemnly. "I had it all taped. Then things started happening too fast. I hadn't time to think properly. Then when the job caught up with me, I lost my head."

"You quite understand that all this is going on the record?"

"I understand all right. I'm going to shop those bastards who dragged me into this. I'll see they go down for it."

"The ones that are left. How did it all start? The Northern Steel job, I mean."

"It was through me, I must admit. I used to go to the bank practically the same time every Friday, and there was the Northern Steel outfit, getting wage money at the same time every week. Just little Verney Barton and a clerk or two, and an old commissionaire. They were sitting ducks. I just waited for somebody to do 'em."

"And when nobody did?"

"Well, I met Gerry Gee. Dad was laid up with his rheumatism, and Gerry came to see why he hadn't been to the club. He said he thought somebody might have offended the old boy, and he wanted to put it right."

"He was a valuable customer, I suppose."

"Well, he was regular. Anyway, after he'd seen the old boy he started selling the club idea to me. I didn't buy it, but he seemed an all-right bloke to me. About a week after that he came round to the shop with some work, some shelves he wanted put up in his office. Well, he's a club type, and they're not good payers. I said I'd see the color of his money for the timber, for a start. He was all right. He just laughed, and said his name was Gee not Gerard."

"I see. Lord Gerard of Northern Steel."

"That's it. There was just him and me talking in the yard, nobody near us. I said somebody was going to take Gerard's firm for plenty one of these days. Then I told him all about it, not thinking anything. My word, he phoned me a month after and asked me to meet him at Arturo's Café. He'd been having a look at the job. He said it was a snip. I was a fool. I should never have gone to meet him."

"You met the others there."

"That's it. I looked at them and they looked at me, and I could see nothing but trouble."

"You had to go into it."

"Yes. You know the rest."

"Not quite. Who did what?"

"Long Cue and Arturo were the drivers. Gerry wanted to be a driver, but he was overruled because Arturo is a bit slow on his feet. He could have got caught if it came to a running job. Cory, Rapp and I did the quietening, and Gerry was the guard in case there was interference. It went off like a dream. Half an hour after we touched, the money was in a special coffin, with a body on top of it. My idea was to bury the money with a body, so's it would be safe till we wanted to dig it up. The trouble was, we didn't have an interment all the time I held that money. We only had cremations, and I had to keep moving the coffin from body to body. That's how my dad eventually tumbled to it."

"Tell me about that later. What went wrong over Verney Barton?"

"Well, we all wore masks, and old clothes. Gerry and Verney knew each other, but Gerry was standby, like I said, and he didn't think he'd be noticed. He wore an old sports coat he used to wear when he was sitting in his office in the daytime or when he had to handle dusty boxes and that. He liked to save his good clothes. Well, this sports coat had a pattern, and a big grease stain on the left lapel."

"And Verney recognized the coat?"

"It was thought so. Verney had money invested in the club, and after the holdup he came to Gerry wanting it out. Said he'd been gambling. Had to pay the bookies or else. Gerry knew he didn't gamble. They were in the office and Gerry was wearing his old coat, and Verney seemed as if he couldn't take his eyes off the grease spot. Gerry fluffed, or thought he did. He guessed Verney was trying to get his money out of the club before he come copper over the holdup."

"So Verney had to be seen off."

"That's it. Rapp and Cory did him, like they did my old man. Long Cue did the driving. I had no hand in it, but it was me who disposed of the body for them. They thought that was a wizard idea."

"It was, too. But for one little thing."

"I know. Gee went and made a charlie of it by stealing the share certificate or whatever you'd call it. He ruined the whole thing with that. That's why I'm shopping the greedy bastard. Cory was real mad about that. He was ready to kill Gerry."

"I'll bet he was. Now, what about the coffin?"

"Oh, that was awful. That Saturday afternoon the old lad walked into the Chapel of Rest just when I had the coffin empty. Empty but for the money in the bottom, I mean. As luck had it, the blasted lid was off too. He looked into it, and it looked to him as if it hadn't a proper waterproof lining. That was the false bottom, you see. Then he noticed the big difference between measurements outside and in and began asking questions. Then it was amazing how quick he twigged what was on. I looked as guilty as hell, I expect. Anyway, there it was. Dad didn't mind upping somebody's bill a bit, but he wouldn't have aught to do with stealing. He said he'd give me twenty-four hours to get that money back to the rightful owners, as how I did it. Then he walked out and left me with it."

"Quite a dilemma for you."

"It was a hell of a dilemma. I didn't want to give up that money after I'd taken so much trouble to get it. Besides, I couldn't. However I handled it, Cory or Long Cue would figure out what I'd done. My life wouldn't have been worth tuppence. Well, there was an arrangement for Cory to phone me every day, from a different phone box. I told him what had happened. He was very cool about it. He said he'd have a talk with the old boy, and whitewash me and say I'd been forced into it. Then he'd convince him he'd better keep quiet for his own sake and mine. He said he could make him see reason without laying a finger on him. So we arranged it so our housekeeper would phone Dad at the club, and Cory could be waiting for him when he came to pick up a laying-out board."

"You set it up."

"I set it up." Ben's voice broke. In his weakness he began to cry. Except for the sound of his weeping the room was quiet.

Nobody looked at him. Eventually he dried his eyes with the back of his hand and spoke in a harsher voice. "It's time I stopped kidding," he said. "I set it up, and kidded myself it was going to be all right. But I knew in my heart all along they were going to kill him without giving him a chance to say a word. I knew, all right. Cory got through to me the day after and said Dad started to raise a yell, and Rapp did it before he could stop him. I don't know if that's true or not."

"It was Cory's knife."

"Ah. Bloody murderers, the pair of 'em."

"Who got Cory and Lancaster out of the cells?"

"Rapp and me. Then Rapp got the bright idea they'd all kip down in the Chapel of Rest. Stupid idiot."

"Not so nice for you. Who thought of doing the Drill Hall?"

"Rapp. When they got the griff about Dixie Costello they all went scatty. That's when I started to realize it couldn't go on. I had to quieten that lot to save myself."

"You certainly quietened them. Care to tell me about it?"

"What's the point?"

"Just to keep the records tidy. It can't affect you one way or the other."

Ben sighed. "No, I suppose it can't." He obliged with an account of the last hours of Cory, Lancaster and Rapp. Martineau listened to the dreadful story in silence. "If that bobby hadn't appeared on the scene, you'd never have had the faintest idea what happened to those three," he concluded.

"You could be right. But one of my boys twigged the idea of the coffin boat. That was one of your better ones, balancing it with a six-foot length of wood, with a two-gallon can clamped to each end."

"Yes. But it was slow work. You found the coffin?"

"In the woodshed at the White Swan. And we found the guns in the canal."

"Eileen didn't know the coffin was there. She's a good girl. She didn't know I'd come along the canal, and she didn't know about the money."

Martineau had his own ideas about that, but he let the matter go by. He had too much to do already. There was a host of prisoners to be charged with a bookful of crimes; a great deal of paper work; new jobs coming up. The criminal element of Granchester had not been standing still while he had been engaged with his robbery-murder case.

"Dixie Costello led us to the White Swan," he said. "How did he get the word on that, do you think?"

"There's a little bookie's runner sometimes goes into the taproom at the Swan. He might have known about me, maybe, and tipped off Dixie."

Martineau nodded, reflecting on the range and efficiency of Costello's intelligence service. Somehow he had learned quite early in the day that Ben was wanted by the police. A leak from inside the force? Possibly. Anyway, he would be very busy on the telephone after that.

The chief inspector looked at the man whose idle speculations concerning robbery had started the bloodiest chain of crimes that had ever happened in the city. He wondered what a prison psychiatrist would make of him.

Ben seemed to read his thoughts. "I went haywire at the finish," he said. "I didn't have time to stop and think."

Again Martineau let it go with a nod. At no time had Ben expressed any sympathy for innocent people who had suffered at the hands of himself and his accomplices. He had only been sorry about his father, and now no doubt he was sorry for himself. He was prime gallows meat.

When the chief constable sent for him, Martineau wondered a little. It was not yet the time for commendations. Had some sort of trouble blown up?

It was not trouble for Martineau, at any rate. The great man greeted him amiably. "Sit down, chief inspector," he said. "You've been working very hard. And successfully, as usual."

Martineau sat down. "Yes, sir," he said. "Thank you, sir."

"I have here the application of a P. C. Ainslie for transfer to the C.I.D. It is recommended by you. Well, you seem to pick your men very well. I have approved the application."

"Very good, sir." So that wasn't it. And what was a document of that sort doing on the Old Man's desk, anyway?

But now the chief was frowning. He said, "Ainslie has made

two applications, and it is the second one I'm concerned about. He wants to get married, and he has applied for one of the new police houses at Honey Green."

"Why not, sir? Most of us do get married."

"Ah, yes. He states here that the young woman is a dressmaker, but Chief Superintendent Clay informs me that she is a—a cabaret dancer. In a night club, as a matter of fact."

"She is a dressmaker, sir. She *was* a dancer, until quite recently."

"H'm. You know that I believe a happy and tranquil home life is essential for a policeman. Would a girl with this sort of background settle down all right? Surely when she's lived this so-called glamorous life she won't make a suitable wife for a constable?"

Martineau could have agreed. Suppose the marriage did go on the rocks? There was no need for him to risk official displeasure over such an event. But Ainslie was a good man. Furthermore, he was, or would be, one of Martineau's men. And Martineau believed in looking after his own.

"It could be as you say, sir," he replied. "But I know the young lady. I met her in the line of duty, and so did Ainslie. She went out of her way and put herself into danger to help the police. She did it purely as a public duty, I think. She is a nice girl, of good character, intelligent, courageous and, I would say, well balanced."

The chief was beaming. "Well, really!" he said. "That is indeed a recommendation. And I can't say I've ever found you to be far wrong in a matter of this sort."

Down came the rubber stamp with the chief's blessing: APPROVED.

>>> If you've enjoyed this book and would like to discover more great vintage crime and thriller titles, as well as the most exciting crime and thriller authors writing today, visit: >>>

The Murder Room
Where Criminal Minds Meet

themurderroom.com

www.ingramcontent.com/pod-product-compliance
Ingram Content Group UK Ltd.
Pitfield, Milton Keynes, MK11 3LW, UK
UKHW041144280225
455666UK00005B/108

9 781471 902758